The Hidden Gardens

Jan Pollard

Eloquent Books

Copyright © 2010

All rights reserved—Jan Pollard

No part of this book may be reproduced or transmitted in any form or by any means, graphic, electronic, or mechanical, including photocopying, recording, taping, or by any information storage retrieval system, without the permission, in writing, from the publisher.

Eloquent Books
An imprint of Strategic Book Group
P.O. Box 333
Durham CT 06422
www.StrategicBookGroup.com

ISBN: 978-1-60911-238-7

Printed in the United States of America

Book Design: Suzanne Kelly

For My Husband Nigel,
A Dedicated Gardener
With Love

"He who plants a garden plants happiness"
$\qquad\qquad\qquad\qquad$ —Chinese Proverb

CHAPTER 1

Mike Fairweather felt cheated. There had been no Millie to feast his eyes upon that morning as she took her child to school.

Perhaps Lucy was unwell. He knew his wife Ruth struck fear into the eight-year-olds she taught at the local primary school, and he felt sure that the excellent reference she had recently received from the head had been given in the hope that she would soon be moving on. Since the arrival of the new baby at Number 6 and the fact that Lucy next door was now in her class it was Ruth's ambition to live elsewhere. It was all she ever talked about, but Mike did not share her feelings on the matter. He wanted to move on, but not with Ruth.

He wondered what he had seen in her when he had asked her to marry him. She had seemed keen enough at the time and he was feeling bruised after a previous relationship had ended when he had met her at a singles evening. She was smart; there was no doubt about that; always dressed to perfection in dark clothes without a hair out of place. Prim was the way he would describe her, prim and proper, a professional woman who could hold her own in company. He supposed that was what he had found attractive about her after taking young women to events that were only sex symbols to boost his own ego.

Jan Pollard

Being an attractive bachelor had begun to wear thin once most of his friends and colleagues had settled down and started families. When Ruth appeared in his life he had felt at the time that she would be an asset but he had been proved wrong. It was too late once he realised that she had set out to catch him, a successful city accountant, two years older than herself, and a man to rely on and to pay the bills. The thought bothered him more than ever now there were no office diversions or attractive secretaries to take his mind off his home life.

His firm had been taken over and rather than face the indignity of taking a back seat and possibly humiliating redundancy he had left and set up a private practice at home while the going was good. Ruth had been agreeable to live in his terrace house in Park Close for a while as it was within walking distance from her school, and with the money they saved from travelling expenses they could eventually afford to have only a small mortgage on a larger house in a better residential area. Mike no longer cared where he lived as long as Ruth was no part of his life. It was a lonely existence but as his room overlooked the Close he could watch the world go by as he worked and that included the gorgeous Millie from next door, for whom he felt an unrequited passion.

Mike was a handsome man in his middle thirties, tall and athletic, with dark brown hair curling at the nape of his neck. His smiling brown eyes were flecked with green and the intensity of his gaze as he gave his full attention to anyone speaking to him made them feel as if they were the only person in the world of importance to him. The warmth of his smile had been the reason for many a cleaner thinking twice about giving in her notice when Ruth had made a complaint about their work.

The letterbox rattled at Number 4 Park Close but Mike was too busy assessing a client's account to be bothered to go downstairs and pick up the post. He had no appetite for work since Millie had not put in her usual appearance but the work had to be done or he would lose his faithful clients for accountants were two a penny these days.

The Hidden Gardens

The front door opened next door and his neighbour Benji stood on the doorstep and kissed his wife Venus as she left for work at the TV studios where she worked. He held their plump baby in his arms and she turned to hug and kiss the child, waving to them as she set off for the tube station. It was a public show of affection which took place every morning and which his own wife deplored; not that she had any affection to give to him.

At his last attempt to get her interested in a bit of lovemaking she had made the forthcoming Ofsted inspections at her school the excuse to deny him her bed; as usual she was just too tired for that kind of thing. Not that he had minded all that much as making love to Ruth was like copulating with a rigid bag of bones and he preferred to sleep without her. She seemed to dislike his very presence in the twin bedded room they shared and he soon found himself relegated to the spare room at the back of the house, which was a relief to them both.

Thankfully they had no children to consider; not that Mike was adverse to fatherhood but Ruth had enough of them during the day and never went near them outside school if she could help it. It would make things easier when the time came to leave.

Mike envied his neighbour and his happy family life. When Benji's booming laughter was heard through the walls and Venus joined in, Mike would smile. Their laughter was infectious and he wished he could get to know them. Benji was often home during the day looking after the baby. They could at least have a nodding acquaintance over the back fence, but Benji rarely went into the back yard apart from emptying the rubbish and Mike had his eyes glued to the computer.

He heard Ruth's key in the lock and called downstairs.

"You're early today aren't you?"

"I told you Mike, but you never listen. We went in for a few hours this morning to prepare for the new term. The kids had an extra day off."

So that was why Millie had not passed under his window that morning. He should have remembered but he rarely listened to what Ruth had to say these days. Her voice seemed to whine with the everlasting problems of her job and he had become immune to it.

"You haven't even picked up the post yet."

Mike sighed; another complaint from his wife.

"Is there anything interesting?"

"Just the usual rubbish and a letter from a television channel. They would like to do a makeover on the back garden *and* pay us too as long as we help a bit."

Mike came downstairs.

"Are we going to make some money from it?"

"That's what I was thinking. Would you have time to help? I couldn't do anything now the term has started. It might get you out in the fresh air for a bit. You're always stuck behind that computer."

"But why us? Why did they choose us? There are far worse back gardens along here."

"It's everyone in Park Close—all six houses although I doubt if that poor old thing in the corner house will co-operate; probably never reads her post. She looks more dead than alive when you catch a glimpse of her shuffling out of her house dressed in those awful clothes, carrying that dirty old bag. I've begun to think she must be a squatter; surely it's not her property."

"I doubt it. She's been there for as long as I can remember."

"Well, everyone has a right to live as they choose but she lowers the tone of the Close. Someone ought to report her to the Social Services so she is taken away."

Mike looked at his wife. She was a heartless woman. He pitied the children in her care. Perhaps his life would change if they took up this offer. He might get to know some of his neighbours instead of being on a nodding acquaintance; especially Millie, next door to them at Number 2. His heart missed a beat. He had watched her enough times taking her little girl to school in the mornings and bringing her back in the afternoons. The child, Lucy, was in Ruth's class so he knew Millie was a single parent. Ruth had told him that Millie Carrington's parents were dead and she had been left the house.

The Hidden Gardens

"She's no better than she should be," was Ruth's opinion of their neighbour. "You must have seen those young men going into her house and coming out again in the mornings. I expect she sleeps with them. Lucy has no father."

"Oh Ruth! That's rubbish. I know for a fact that she takes in students. I saw the last ones going into the School of Languages the other day when I was passing."

Ruth pursed her lips and made no reply to that observation. She hated to be proved wrong.

"Let's change the subject shall we? What are we going to do with this letter?"

"I'm happy to go along with it. We might get more for the house if the garden has been seen on TV."

"Right—I'll leave you to sort it out then."

Mike went back upstairs to write a reply, seething inwardly. How dare his wife make such spiteful remarks about a poor woman trying to make a decent living for herself. He had often thought about Millie Carrington since one, never to be forgotten evening, as he had put the cat out he had seen her silhouetted against the blind in the back bedroom of the house next door. She had taken off her blouse and then her bra and had stretched up her arms and arched her back in a luxurious stretch before switching off the light. For a few seconds Mike had seen the shape of her firm round breasts and pointed nipples and had forgotten everything else until the cat had struggled free from his arms, scratching him in the process. He had never seen her like that again. It had made him feel like a peeping Tom and had disturbed his sleep. He could only think that she lay in her bed on the other side of the wall that divided them and he longed to dissolve through the barrier of brickwork and feel the shadow made into flesh.

It was crazy. His static, sterile life was driving him mad. Now he would have a chance to meet her if she agreed to the makeover. If it was difficult for a young woman on her own with other commitments, then perhaps he could help her with the garden when Ruth was out. They were only small gardens after all.

Wild ideas swam through his head as he thought about it, but he pushed them to one side until he had heard that the project was to go ahead or his feelings would get the better of him.

Millie Carrington opened her back door to let out her last customer for the day, cheerily wishing her goodbye before preparing tea for herself and her daughter. It had been a long day and she felt tired after washing and setting and blow drying, or styling her different customer's hair but she never turned anyone away however difficult it was to fit them in. She needed the money too badly. She had adapted the small outhouse tacked onto the back of the house into a tiny salon with one basin and a mobile hairdryer. One of her lodgers had fixed up a mirror over the basin and had helped to paint the walls a fetching shade of peach. With draped curtains across the garden window, a few hooks for coats and an open weave easy chair she was in business. The lodger who had since left, had been rewarded with free board and lodging for his trouble. Her clients came in through the side gate into the garden. The end houses in the terrace had a passage way which made access easier and helped Millie to keep her business private. She dreaded that awful Mrs Fairweather from next door ever finding out as she might have reported her to the authorities out of spite for not declaring her business for tax purposes and that would have closed her down.

Millie had trained as a hairdresser in one of the West End salons and was good at her job. She had given it up when her mother had died suddenly and her father had become ill with depression and had wasted away. Feeling very vulnerable and lonely she had taken a partner who had left her as soon as he discovered he had made her pregnant and she wanted to keep the baby. Bringing up her child alone she had no time or inclination for any further relationships. Her clients were older women who lived locally and were unable to afford London prices. Some had become good friends to her and were happy to act as surrogate grandparents to Lucy as she grew up and were not averse to doing a little baby sitting. As the years passed and Lucy became old enough for school Millie began to think about finding someone else to share her life with but as yet the right man had not appeared. There had been quite a few offers as she was a beautiful woman with gentle, soulful eyes and a 'little girl lost' expression which men found attractive, but Millie was too nervous to plunge into a relationship again until she felt completely sure the man in her life would accept Lucy. She longed to feel desired again for herself. She knew she turned men's heads as she walked past them and saw the naked lust in their eyes but Millie was looking for more than that; she wanted love.

Lucy looked like a smaller edition of her mother with long, silky blonde hair, large deep blue eyes and a heart shaped face. They were two of a kind with a down to earth attitude to life, taking each day as it came and making the best of it. They did things together and laughed a lot but were shy in company. Millie needed to be sure of people before she wholly trusted them. She adored her daughter; she was, after all, the only person left who belonged to her and she worked hard to provide them both with a decent standard of life.

The foreign students had been a blessing. They shared a double room at the front of the house where there were two single beds, a kettle and a toaster. Lucy had the little room over the front door and Millie slept in the spare room at the back. Girls were not welcome. Millie had soon got tired of losing all her hot water to baths and hair washing. She had enough of that with her own customers. She rarely saw much of the students. They passed like ships in the night; Italians, Indians, Egyptians, whatever—she had given them a roof over their heads and provided them with the means to make hot drinks and snacks and were grateful for their money in return. The School of Languages paid her on a regular basis from the student's grants so she had no problem with that; her only problem at the moment was Lucy's unwillingness to go to school.

Last term Mrs Fairweather seemed to find fault with Lucy over every petty little thing and the child was terrified of her. Millie felt she had been picked on because she was such a quiet inoffensive child who would never say anything in her own defence. Millie would have liked to have given Mrs Fairweather a piece of her mind but as Lucy's teacher lived next door she thought it best to keep a neighbourly distance. It might have made things worse for Lucy. Millie felt sorry for poor Mr Fairweather who had to live with such a harridan. Perhaps she was different at home but somehow she doubted it. He seemed such a nice man and so good looking, working away in his little office above the front door. He gave her the impression of being a very kind person as he smiled cheerfully at them when they set off in the mornings, and he often gave Lucy a wave. Lucy waved back but although Millie smiled up at him she felt it was not her place to wave as well. He might get the wrong idea and that would only add to her present difficulties with his wife and she had enough of them.

"Come on, Lucy. Put your book down—it's tea time."

Lucy reluctantly closed her Harry Potter book and picked up the post from the floor as she went into the kitchen. Of late Lucy examined all the post just in case, like Harry Potter, there was a letter for her inviting her to join another school; any old school would have done, not especially one that taught magic, just a school where Mrs Fairweather no longer taught.

"Another bill, I expect," said Millie as Lucy handed it to her. "You should have left it there, love." Usually Millie only received bills; too many bills which she had trouble paying, or else junk mail which went straight into the dustbin.

"It's not a bill, Mum. It's something to do with Shepherd's Bush. It says so on the back."

"Let's have a look—ah—Shepherd's Bush Studios. It must have come to the wrong house. I expect the postman meant to put it into Number 6. That's where the television lady lives."

"But it's got our address on the envelope, Mum. Look—The Occupier, Number 2, Park Close"

"So it has; whatever can it be?" Millie slit open the envelope and read the contents. "They want to do a makeover of our back garden for a TV programme called, 'In Your Backyard.' Never heard of it have you, Lucy?"

Lucy shook her head.

"They're actually offering us money to do it and if we all agree they'll tell us how much we can have. Just imagine; getting the garden done for nothing!"

"Will you let them, Mum?"

"I should say so—although I'm expected to help as well."

"I'll help," said Lucy, seriously.

"Oh, darling; whatever could you do?"

"You'd be surprised. I could sow some seeds couldn't I? I've always wanted a bit of garden to myself."

Millie hugged her. "You're a great kid. Why didn't you tell me? You could have had some just for yourself. I've hated looking after it ever since your grandpa died; it's hard work; even a little garden like this."

"I only meant a little patch so I could sow some seeds and watch them grow. The pictures on the packets in the shops look so pretty."

"O.K, I'll write to them. You never know; we might be on the telly."

Lucy smiled broadly. "Do you think Mrs Fairweather will be on the telly?"

"She'd crack the screen she would," said Millie, with feeling.

CHAPTER 2

Scrumpi sucked vigorously at her mother's nipple, her huge brown eyes gazing up at her mother's contented face. Venus, who was anxious to get to the studio, changed her baby over to the other breast. "Come on, sweetheart, I haven't got all day. I should have started feeding you a bit earlier."

The baby burped and let go for a minute.

"Right, that's that for now," said Venus putting Scrumpi over her shoulder to get her wind up. "We'll have to put her on solids soon, Benji. Then I can leave her with you all day as long as she'll take a bottle now and again." Venus plonked a kiss on her daughter's nose and proceeded to change her.

Scrumpi made no objection to her milk supply having stopped and looking up at her father blew him some milky bubbles.

"Time for my breakfast now, eh" said Benji. Scrumpi made a loud belching noise in reply and Benji laughed heartily. He never ceased to be fascinated by their unplanned but most welcome child. She was the star in his universe.

"I must get off, Ben. I've got to get to the studio. They want to discuss my plans for reinventing the terrace gardens. I think I can persuade them. It should make for good viewing bringing in the personal tastes of the owners."

"As long as they all agree to the plan; it's not going to work if one of them drops out is it?"

"It's only Edna I'm worried about. She's so rarely seen; goes out all day looking like a tramp and comes back when it's dark. God knows where she gets to all day poor old thing."

"Nobody has set foot into her backyard for years by the look of it. What will you do if you don't hear anything from her?"

"Just work on the other five I suppose. Hers is at the end of the terrace so we could ignore it if it came to the worst. The letters to all the residents should arrive today so we must wait for the feedback and hope we don't have to wait for too long. I'm fairly sure the man next door might be interested as he works from home and so does that pretty young woman at the end, the one with the little girl, but it might be too much for her as she lives on her own apart from her lodgers. Let's wait and see."

Benji shrugged in reply. His wife was full of ideas. She sub-edited the television programme, 'Looking at Your Backyard,' and they needed something to give the programme a lift. New ideas were in short supply where gardening programmes were concerned and Venus was confident she could talk them round when they realised it was to take the form of a real live soap opera, with the residents lives of as much importance as their gardens. There was to be a cash incentive and the residents would be told exactly what was expected of them at a general meeting in their house. Improvements would be made to their gardens, providing some physical help was forthcoming from those who were able to help otherwise there would have to be an adjustment to the amount each household received. A little animosity between the neighbours or a new friendship arising from the project would all add spice to the programme, as long as they were willing to express their thoughts on camera. It was a bold venture on her part but if it worked it should appeal to the addicts of soap operas who never usually bothered to look at gardening programmes.

Venus handed Scrumpi to her father before she left. Benji was in charge of the baby for the morning.

"Hey," called out Benji as he followed her to the door. "What about breakfast? Don't I get any?"

"None left," laughed Venus. "Your daughter's had it all."

Benji was a chef at Rowlands Hotel in the Barbican. He had known Venus all his life. Their grand parents had come from Jamaica on the same boat to make their fortunes in the big city and then found there was no fortune to be made and had eked out an existence for their families. Their children had done a little better for themselves and the next generation had made their way by dogged perseverance into their own careers. Venus was the first to find the job she wanted after working in a club as a waitress. Here she met a television presenter after chatting to him about her aim in life which was to work in a film studio. She was so enthusiastic that he found her a position in the canteen at Shepherd's Bush studios where her never ending cheerfulness endeared her to everybody. Her ideas for programmes were just a joke to the presenters and producers who met her while ordering meals until one day someone took notice and realised she had promise. From that day onwards she was treated as a member of the team and her bright, intelligent ideas were no longer considered as a joke. At present she was the sub-editor of a gardening series knowing very little about gardening herself but she knew where to make cuts in programmes to the best effect and was well liked by the TV crews and presenters.

Scrumpi's arrival had been an unexpected blip in their plans for the future but things had turned out well. Benji usually worked in the evenings and cared for Scrumpi during the day when Venus was out. At thirty years of age he was no longer treated as an underdog in the kitchens where he had learned his trade. Benji had a gentle nature within his powerful frame and those who did not know him were not keen on picking a fight in case they lost the contest. His cooking skills and his unflappable nature in the hot atmosphere of many a kitchen soon earned him the respect he deserved and he was eagerly sought after by the best hotels.

Venus had put his name forward as a chef for a television show once he had become an expert on Jamaican cuisine and his genial manner and throaty laugh as he cracked jokes had made him popular with the audiences. She had suggested he wrote a cookery book on his specialist subject. The first book took off and now there was to be a second. He wrote his recipes while Scrumpi slept or gurgled in her basket. It was a blessing to have such a good contented baby. Benji hoped to become as famous as other TV cooks and now sported a hairstyle to go with his Jamaican roots. Look what Gary Rhodes' hairstyle had done for him! He was always recognised immediately and that was what Benji was aiming for. He was so proud of his beautiful plump Venus with her happy disposition and her hips which swayed from side to side as she walked, her big brown sultry eyes and her lips like red hot peppers. Now her breasts were like huge melons, full of nourishment for their child. She was almost good enough to eat. He would make up a recipe just for her, using dark and white chocolate and call it Scrumptious in honour of the baby they had made together. Just thinking about her beautiful brown body took his mind off the recipe and it wasn't until Scrumpi needed a bit of attention that he got round to writing something down.

At the studio in Shepherd's Bush Venus had explained the lay out of the terrace and the universal size of the long gardens which finished at the railway line. There was general approval for her idea. It was to be different from the usual makeover programmes which were now beginning to lose audiences, as the residents would all have a say in the planning, and with the professionals there as well to be a link with their everyday lives to keep the viewers interest alive from week to week, it would become a real life soap opera. They would earn their hand out from the television company; Venus would see to that as she was to organise the whole project.

The follow up book on the series would feature each household and they would benefit financially from those which would be an added incentive to take part.

Julian Goodwood and Beatrice Thorn were chosen to be the presenters, should all the residents be agreeable to the idea.

"We'll never do it for £10, 000," grumbled the producer, Ed. "More like £100,000 plus, if we're lucky. No fancy ideas in the gardens like expensive statuary. Julian and Beatrice command high salaries these days and that would have to be found from somewhere."

"It will work out, I'm sure of it." Venus was anxious not to see her idea thrown out.

"There will be six programmes, spread over the six different gardens, and a final programme when everyone comes together, with an open day for the public to come and view the work. We can also have a viewers 'phone in' at the end to vote for the best garden, and with all the gardening adverts we can push in we will make a profit. Involving the public so they feel a part of the programme is good for television."

"Doesn't one of the gardens belong to you?" asked a voice from the back.

Venus recognised the girl who was angling for her job and flashed her a wide smile.

"Oh, yes. That's where I got the idea from. I shall be on the spot to stop their interest from flagging."

Nobody else objected and it was agreed to reconsider the idea when the answers were returned.

Venus left for home, ignoring the trouble maker at the back and hurried back to see to her baby. It would be so much easier once she was working from home part time; a fact which had never been far from her mind.

"I suppose the railway line at the end of these gardens will give us some privacy," remarked the producer. "It's a long project and onlookers would get in the way."

"Not to mention the trains on the Central Line passing at regular intervals to liven things up," said a voice from the back.

The producer, who was fond of Venus, and found her easy to work with, ignored the girl who had spoken. Up to now all of the suggestions Venus had come up with had been winners and he trusted her judgement. The only thing that bothered him was making a profit on such a huge investment. Losing money would be a disaster for the company.

Venus and Benji had never done much about their own garden apart from a general tidy up a few times a year, and the weeds flourished amongst the dusty borders. This had troubled their neighbours when unwanted seeds blew onto their patch, as Guy de Courcy and Damian Wentworth were fussy people.

Guy ran a Gay Club in Pimlico, where he had met Damian a year ago. They had many interests in common, apart from their preference for the male sex; good food, excellent wine and a love of fine antiques being high on their list. Damian managed a select bookshop in Westminster, where only highly expensive books with elegant bindings were on prominent display, leaving the more popular titles on the shelves to be discovered by the browsing public. In the back room were kept a supply of more explicit books for club members only. The profits from the club kept the elegant Westminster Book World afloat, despite the closure of small bookshops in the area. It was a constant problem with the competition from the big book stores and the public preference for the television classics. People no longer read books as they had done in the past now television and computer games had taken their place.

Damian was twenty years older than his partner Guy, and set in his ways. He had lived with his elderly mother until she had died, a cantankerous, difficult woman in her old age when suffering from arthritis. Unknown to Damian she had altered her Will a few years before her death, leaving her money to a distant relative, after Damian had refused to comply with one of her more petty requests. Damian had been shocked to discover her ingratitude after all his years of care, and had been obliged to move from his comfortable home in Richmond into the terrace house in Park Close which was all he could afford. His mother's elegant antique furniture and fine china were all that had been left to him and were his only source of comfort until he had met Guy.

Guy had altered everything. He was intensely sociable, good looking, and always well dressed. Damian noticed him when he had visited the book shop and had made enquiries about the book club. After a short conversation Guy had left a card advertising the Gay Club with Damian.

"You'll find me serving behind the bar," Guy had said, giving Damian a wink.

Damian had gone that evening and had found it hard to stop talking to Guy about his possessive mother and his loneliness. Things soon changed after that. Guy, whose last lover had moved on, soon moved in with Damian and they became inseparable. Damian had discovered love for the first time in his life.

Guy was good at gardening and cooking, and Damian kept the house impeccably tidy, polishing the antique furniture 'just the way Mummy had always liked it,' as he used to tell Guy, much to his annoyance.

"Forget the past, Damian. Get it out of your system," he would say, irritably. "I'm here now. Be happy."

And Damian would do just that. He was happy; happier than he had ever been, that is until the letter from the television company had dropped onto the mat of Number 8 Park Close. Guy picked it up and read it.

"Listen to this, Dame. It's from the producer of that gardening programme, 'Looking at Your Backyard.' They want to make a programme about The Close. What do you think of that, for goodness sake? They're even offering money to improve our back gardens, would you believe; possibly six or seven programmes."

Damian left the washing up and came into the hallway.

"Perhaps they think our backyard needs some improvement," he said, with a cutting edge to the remark, knowing that Guy was proud of his gardening prowess.

"Cheeky!" Guy supposed it was one of Damian's doubtful remarks and refused to get riled.

"There's money in it if we agree. It might be fun. All those brawny men they'll bring in to do the digging, with their muscles rippling. I can't wait!"

This type of repartee was Guy's way of getting his own back on his lover. Damian was still reading the letter. "We'll have to do some of the work ourselves; did you read that bit? They don't give us the money for nothing."

"Not your scene, more mine. I'd need a say in what went on in my patch. It's worth thinking about though; we'd be on the telly. Good for business."

"I suppose so, now you mention it. The shop isn't exactly flourishing. They bring out books about all these series. I could make a prominent display in the window and mention our involvement."

"Good idea—so what do you think?"

"Give me a few days to think it over."

Guy's remark about the brawny men and their physical attributes had rattled him slightly. If Guy left him for a younger or more virile partner Damian thought he would die. Guy had become his reason for living.

"Why have they chosen our terrace, do you think?"

"I can't imagine. Perhaps because the next door's garden is full of weeds and Edna's on the end is a rubbish tip. A challenge I suppose."

"Ah yes, next door." Damian had a sudden thought. "Venus works for a television company doesn't she?"

"That's it—of course, our black Madonna. I'll bet she thought of it so someone would come and makeover her garden."

Both men chuckled. It was so like Venus somehow. They had been alarmed at first when Venus had produced a child, concerned that their peace would be shattered at night by a crying baby. But Scrumpi was a perfect baby who rarely grizzled and their fears had come to nothing. Venus and Benji were friendly good neighbours, and since Benji had featured in the programme, 'Cook It My Way' and had produced a book of recipes which sold well in Damian's shop they had become good friends. Guy and Damian had visited the restaurant in the Barbican for a meal. Benji had been flattered and the friendship had flourished, especially as Guy was a keen cook and they had an interest in common.

Guy picked up the 'phone. "I'll give Benji a buzz and see if Venus is behind this."

When Benji answered and assured them that Venus had thought up the idea they decided immediately to agree to the plan.

"Great, man!" boomed Benji, with his hearty laugh. "Venus will be thrilled when I tell her." He put down the 'phone and smiled. Just four more to go

CHAPTER 3

"What the hell's that!" Malcolm was gazing out of the back window of Number 10, Park Close, at a large garment pegged to the line in the next door's back yard. 'Garden' was too respectable a description for the nettle patch through which various rusty objects were to be seen; bicycle handlebars, a pram, old dustbins and a shopping trolley, to name but a few.

Linda put down her paintbrush to come and look.

"Good God! Edna's done some washing!!"

"What are they for heavens sake—her bloomers?"

"I reckon so. First time in all the years we've been here that I've ever seen anything on her line. What's come over her?"

"Perhaps she had an accident." Malcolm laughed, unkindly.

"Oh, Malcolm, the poor old thing; I feel so sorry for her. I offered to take her stuff to the launderette for her the other day, when I saw her going out. I told her I'd do them for free." Linda was manageress of the launderette in the parade of shops close by. She ran the business on her own without any other staff, but considered herself to be the manageress, especially if there were any complaints.

"You never said. What did she say?"

"She said she didn't want any charity, so I haven't bothered her since."

The Hidden Gardens

Malcolm continued to splash buttercup yellow paint on the wall. "You can't help some people, especially her sort."

"No, but someone ought to. She needs help."

"Where did she come from, for goodness sake? The house was empty when we came to live here and now the front door is off its hinges and two of the windows are broken. The landlord should do something about it. It's a disgrace to the Close. Those two blokes next door have tried to find the owner without success. You know how fussy they are. It lets down the tone of the place; at least we all try to keep our properties looking respectable."

"Well, we own them don't we, or some people are paying a mortgage for theirs. We only got this one so cheap because of the state of Number 12, and if it had been as bad as it is now I don't think I would have considered buying this at all."

Linda sighed. It was a problem to be sure, but with property the price it was now they were fortunate to live so close to Malcolm's work, maintaining the railway lines into the City. Soon their daughter, Alice, would be leaving the comprehensive school and moving in with her boyfriend who, in Linda's opinion was far too old for her, and that would leave William at home. The constant bickering between their two children had made life anything but peaceful. Things would improve once Alice had a life of her own, or so she hoped.

"We'll never be able to sell this even if we want to unless something is done about the house on the end."

"Well it's odd you should say that. This morning a letter arrived from a film company. They want to makeover all the gardens in the Close so that means Edna's as well. Perhaps they'll find the owner. You can do a lot by advertising for people to come forward on the telly."

"You might be right. Let's look at that letter."

Linda went downstairs to fetch it. She hadn't intended to mention it until Malcolm had settled down to watch the television one evening and was in a good mood. His vegetables meant so much to him that any interference from anybody would never be tolerated. Every year he dug over their entire plot and planted an assortment of vegetables, but potatoes predominated, early ones in particular. He had never had any time for flowers which he considered a waste of space, and the extra vegetables brought in a small amount of income. Malcolm sold them to his mates at work and used the money to have a flutter on the horses and for the occasional night out at the pub. It was his money and Linda never objected to how he spent it. She earned herself a little extra at bingo, when she was lucky, to spend on herself. With two teenagers to feed Malcolm's efforts in the garden helped a bit with the housekeeping and now Alice was leaving home it would ease things a bit.

Malcolm read the letter quickly.

"I don't want anyone messing my veggies about, Linda. Our garden is fine as far as I am concerned."

"Oh, come on, Malcolm. If it means getting Edna's patch cleared it will be worth it. We would become famous and people might take an interest in buying our house when we think of selling. I don't want to go on living here once you've retired, although I know that's a long time off yet."

"Good God woman. I'm only forty! What are you talking about?"

Linda smiled. She knew she was being ridiculous but time passed only too quickly these days. She was finding it a pain to find trousers large enough to encompass her ever widening hips and yet when she had married Malcolm she was only a slip of a girl and that didn't seem so long ago. She would soon be middle aged and the thought terrified her.

Malcolm read the letter again. His wife had a point he supposed.

"Well, if we agree to this crack brained idea, who's going to help do the garden next door? Edna? Think about it, Linda. For more years than I can remember that garden has been a tip, and I'm not offering my services."

Linda thought for a moment. "William might help."

Malcolm roared with laughter. "William!! You're out of your mind. He can't even pick up a pair of jeans off the floor to help himself. You've spoilt him since birth."

Linda flushed. "No I haven't. It's just his age. All boys of his age only think about themselves. If we paid him for doing it perhaps he'd take an interest—he's always asking me for money. He never seems to have enough although you give him an allowance."

"Take an interest! William! My arse!"

"Be fair. You never know."

Malcolm looked at her pityingly. She had a mother's faith in her only son and never saw him for what he was, a selfish teenager; a layabout who took no more notice of his father than a fly on the wall.

"Well I'll write to them, or better still, I'll 'phone. I don't like writing letters but if it means getting Edna's patch tidied up then I'll agree; as long as I can keep my veggies."

Linda smiled. After considerable grumbling from her spouse she usually ended up getting her own way. Malcolm began to wash out his paint brush. He had finished one wall in Alice's bedroom and the others could wait. Linda had some mad idea that by painting her daughter's bedroom a buttercup yellow, her favourite colour, Alice might have second thoughts about leaving home at sixteen but it had made no difference. Alice was going to pastures new with her forty year old lover. Linda was confident that she might return when she got tired of him and the endless chore of keeping house, but Malcolm thought otherwise. Life would be a lot quieter once she had gone, and he would be glad to see the back of William as well if he ever got tired of having a willing slave to run about for him and feed him, but somehow he had his doubts. William knew which side his bread was buttered, and kept well in with his mother.

"Time for me to be off then; I won't be back until the morning; the last shift finishes at six. All this overtime since that dreadful accident has been a blessing in some ways but I'd rather work in daylight hours and get a good night's sleep."

Malcolm picked up his lunch box, kissed his wife and made tracks for the front door. He could walk to the station at Hanger Lane from Park Close and take a train to wherever along the line the work was taking place. His travel was free as he worked for

Jan Pollard

the London Underground system so there were no expenses in getting to work.

"Don't forget to make that 'phone call," Linda shouted after him, but he had gone. She would have to make it or it would never get done, and Linda wanted these television people to come and talk to Malcolm about the back garden. Perhaps they could persuade him to build a patio near the back door so she could have a few pots of flowers to look after. She had asked Malcolm enough times about it but he had no interest in paying out good money for slabs and pots when the park was only across the road. She could sit in the park and smell the flowers any time she wanted, was his usual reply. Not that Linda had much time for sitting down anyway with the family to look after and her job at the launderette, but it would have made a change from looking at all the vegetables from the kitchen window when she was washing up.

The view from the front windows of the houses in Park Close was a pleasant one. Originally there had been a similar row of houses on the other side of the street, numbered in odd numbers, until a bomb during the last war, had fallen in the park behind them and had demolished the entire row. The even numbered houses had also suffered damage but not to the extent that they could not be repaired. Park Close had become a cul-de-sac away from the main road and the constant roar of traffic and overlooked the green acres and trees of the park beyond. The bomb crater had been made into a pond with a fountain and surrounded by flower beds. It would have been an almost perfect place to live apart from the rattle of trains passing so close to the houses on the Central Line, but like most things the residents had got used to the noise in time. There was room to park their cars on the greensward that edged the pavement on the opposite side of the road, and Malcolm parked his old rust bucket there permanently but Mike Fairweather preferred to keep his in the lock up garage a few streets away. Venus and Benji had no car at present and Damian could not afford a garage and was too fussy to leave a car unattended on the other side of the road and anyway he preferred to take the train or use the many buses

The Hidden Gardens

which travelled along Acton Lane, which was within walking distance. Guy would have liked a car but up to now had relied on his lover's cars until he met Damian, and was in the process of trying to persuade Damian if he would agree to buying one between them.

Having made the 'phone call to the studio Linda tidied up the paint things and set off for the supermarket to buy some necessities. Mondays were her day off. Mike saw her walking past, her hair a burnished auburn today. He could have sworn that the last time he had seen Linda she had been a brassy blonde. She always gave the appearance of being thrown together, wearing the first thing that came to hand. So different from his own too perfect wife. Linda wore a harassed expression as if life was getting her down and Mike felt some sympathy for her, feeling as he did about his own life. The squabbling between the Collins' children had on occasion been heard by all the residents of the Close when it had spilled out onto the street.

Mike's wife, Ruth, had heard that Alice Collins was the mistress of the science master at the comprehensive school, and him as old as her father. He had been suspended although they had both denied the relationship. Alice was leaving at the end of term when she would be sixteen and was no doubt joining her lover in Wales where he had obtained a new job. Science teachers were short on the ground and schools could not afford to be too fussy about such matters but the family must have suffered over the disgrace. Sometimes he was glad that he and Ruth were a childless couple although the delightful baby next door made him feel differently. Venus and Benji appeared to be perfect parents; completely wrapped up in their happy little child.

In the supermarket Linda saw a packet of jam tarts and put them in amongst her shopping to give to Edna. Occasionally she would give her some small item of food or leave it just inside the half open front door. Edna had been ungracious on every occasion saying that she wanted none of Linda's charity, but had taken it nevertheless which is why Linda persevered. Malcolm would probably have called her a silly old fool, and to mind her own business so Linda never told him. It had been on the first occasion that she had met Edna going into the house next door that she had asked Edna her name, telling her that she, Linda, was her neighbour. It had been many years ago when Edna had seemed a bit more forthcoming. She had just muttered her name and that was all Linda had ever got out of her. Edna lived in a world of her own and where she had come from nobody knew.

"There's only Edna," said Venus on her arrival back home. "We've heard from everyone else in the terrace, so we've decided to go ahead with the project. I'll *try* to speak to her about it but I doubt if I shall get anywhere."

"She's only a squatter isn't she? So what does she matter? It would be a shame to spoil your grand idea just for Edna." Benji felt sorry for his wife. She had put so much work into her idea for a programme and the two garden designers had agreed to take part.

The other participants were to be invited to a meeting in their house at Number 6 to discuss the type of garden they would like to help create, and to meet the designers, Julian Goodwood and Beatrice Thorn.

"I'll go round now. She seems to come home about this time of day. She should be told about it. She might be frightened if she saw a lot of strange men clearing out her rubbish and digging and planting round the back of her house. We should tell her in case she calls in the police to stop the work. Nobody knows if she has any rights to the property"

"Only squatters' rights; she's been there for a long time. Bear that in mind when you talk to her, Venus."

Venus nodded and set off to see Edna. Pushing open the ill fitting door Venus was aware of the letter addressed to the occupier stuck under the door frame and picked it up with a whole pile of junk mail that was on the step, and knocked. There was no reply so she called out Edna's name. There was a sound from above; a harsh rasping cough and then silence.

"Is that you, Edna? Are you all right?"

There was no reply, just silence. Venus felt frustrated and after a few minutes she went round to Number 10 and knocked.

Linda opened the door in amazement. She had never expected to find the exotic Venus on her doorstep. Wearing a bright orange skirt and purple blouse with an orange and green turban on her head Venus looked as if she should be on a tropical island. Linda felt uplifted by the sight of her.

"Sorry to bother you, but it's about your neighbour."

"Edna?"

"Yes. I wanted to tell her about the plans to dig up and replant her backyard, but I can't raise her. There seems to be someone there but they don't answer. We wrote to her but she hasn't replied; in fact the letter is still on her step."

"That doesn't surprise me at all. I don't think she knows what's going on to tell you the truth—poor Edna."

"I'm glad *you* agree to it though. It should be good fun and make a lot of difference to the terrace. Oh, I'm Venus by the way, from Number 6. You'll be seeing a lot of me once the project gets going."

"That'll be nice," said Linda, feeling at a loss as to what to say. She had no idea that the lady with the baby had anything to do with this television programme until then and it came as a bit of a shock. She hoped Malcolm wouldn't mind when she told him she had made the 'phone call and discovered that Venus was arranging it. Malcolm only trusted men to make important arrangements and his vegetable garden was the most important thing in the whole world to him. Linda had often thought that if she could have been a prize cabbage her husband would have taken more notice of her.

"You won't forget to mention it to Edna, will you?" said Venus, as she left.

"I'll try—but I can't be sure that she'll listen."

Linda closed the door and leaned up against it. She dreaded telling Malcolm when he came home. There would be yet another row. He would have forgotten about the letter from the television company by the time he arrived back from work, tired and ready for his bed. He had only just recovered from his fury when he had first heard about their Alice and her decision to

Jan Pollard

go off with her science teacher once she had left school, and when he discovered he was as old as himself all hell had been let loose. Linda felt as if she was coming apart at the seams. If it hadn't been for their William who still needed her she would have set up home in the launderette just for a bit of peace.

CHAPTER 4

Millie looked around her and admired the beech units and the spotless surfaces of the modern kitchen she could see through an archway. Venus and Benji had opened up their house from front to back, doing away with the small rooms and turning it into a large open living area. It had an airy, uncluttered appearance with plenty of room for the residents of the Close when they gathered for their meeting. Large colourful cushions lay on the polished floor in the place of seats when the chairs were filled and Millie was sitting on one of them. Lucy had stayed at home. If Mrs Fairweather was going to be at the meeting then Lucy had no wish to be present.

Having been the first to arrive Millie had the opportunity to watch her neighbours as they came through the door and found themselves a seat. She recognised them by sight yet could not put a name to them all. People moved frequently these days without giving her a chance to get to know them. The Fairweathers had only lived next door to her for a few years. The house had belonged to Mike originally but he was rarely in residence during his bachelor days. Now he worked from home she saw him through his office window but she had never spoken to his wife as she appeared not to want to know her neighbours. It had been different during the days of her childhood when people had been friendlier and everyone in the Close had known everyone else. Times had changed and people kept to themselves. Perhaps the garden scheme would bring them all together which would be a good thing.

When the Fairweathers arrived Mike gave her a friendly smile before sitting on a chair close by. Millie smiled back shyly and bent her head as his wife sat down; she wanted to avoid eye contact with the woman who had made her Lucy's life such a misery. Dressed in black trousers with a skinny black top and her black hair pulled into a tight chignon at the nape of her head, Millie thought Ruth resembled a thin black pencil. Her bright red lipstick and her long red fingernails painted to match, gave her the appearance of a haughty model as she sat stiffly in her chair. There seemed to be no warmth in her to interact with a child and Millie felt a pang of sympathy for Lucy and her classmates having to face such a hard faced woman each school day. Compared to his wife Mike was totally relaxed. Wearing a brown check shirt and baggy brown corduroys he smiled genially at the assembled company. Every so often he stole a look at Millie sitting curled up on a big fat cushion as if she had been transported from a sultan's harem, hiding behind the silk curtain of her blonde, almost flaxen hair. In her pale blue denims with a short blue top which showed her midriff, and wearing gold sandals on her tiny feet, Mike could hardly take his eyes off her. She was everything he had imagined her to be and he desired her even more now she was so close to him.

Linda Collins and her husband, Malcolm, made a noisy entrance as she pulled him inside when he looked as if he was about to leave, given half a chance. A thickset man with a shaved head and an angry expression on his face it was only too obvious he had come under sufferance, persuaded by his spiky red headed wife. Millie recognised them as the noisy family who had been overheard by everyone in the Close when their voices had spilled out of their open windows during their brawls. Millie had seen Linda in the launderette where she was the manageress, when she took in her lodger's sheets for washing. Linda always wore clothes that were too young for her age

The Hidden Gardens

and too tight for her figure and changed her hair styles to match. She usually looked worn down and harassed which was not surprising when you saw her husband.

Behind them came Guy and Damian from Number 8 who slid quietly and almost unobserved into the seats behind Ruth. Guy, who was the shorter, had a red silk scarf tucked into the neck of his shocking pink silk shirt, and a red silk handkerchief to match in the pocket. Both men wore matching well cut cream trousers and Damian sported a gold chain over his more conventional outfit. Guy was completely at ease with his flamboyant appearance and sat down with a flourish, as if he was on stage. Damian smiled politely at everyone and settled himself in a less obvious manner. There was a sudden silence as if a play was about to begin as the assembled company took stock of these reclusive neighbours.

Once all of the residents had arrived, apart from Edna, whom nobody had expected to come, Ed, the producer of the series, handed them each a glass of wine, and when they had settled, Benji came round with a plate of his spice biscuits on which he was complimented, much to his satisfaction. Not to be outdone by his wife, who was dressed in a long skirt patterned with red and purple hibiscus flowers and a yellow top for the occasion, Benji was resplendent in a shirt patterned with brightly coloured parrots sitting amongst palm trees. His wide smile and obvious pleasure at meeting them all put everyone at their ease, and Scrumpi's happy chuckles as she sat in her high chair brought a smile to most faces.

Ed shook hands all round and expressed his delight that the people of the Close had shown such co-operation for the scheme; the only exception being Edna, and once everyone was settled he introduced Julian Goodwood and Beatrice Thorn to the assembled company.

"If anyone has any preference for any type of garden or an objection to any of our suggestions please let us know before the end of the meeting," said Julian, a man in his late twenties with tow coloured hair, wearing fashionable pale blue chinos and an open necked shirt to match. Malcolm disliked him on sight. He didn't look as if he had ever lifted a spade to dig a trench in his life, but then appearances could be deceptive. Where had he got such a tan at this time of the year? Not in our present climate, that's for sure.

"Beatrice and I have drawn up some ideas as all your gardens are of a universal size but for the sake of the programme we plan to make each garden quite different. We would like you to look at them now and then let us know which appeals to you. Take your time; we don't want to put any pressure on you."

Beatrice Thorn, a stocky woman in well worn jeans and a white blouse then passed copies of their designs to everyone. With her short, no nonsense hair style and her rough hands she gave the appearance of a dedicated gardener, and quite the opposite of her colleague, Julian.

Venus came round to refill their glasses and put them all at ease as everyone began to talk amongst themselves.

"There isn't anything about vegetables here," said Malcolm, indignantly. "All this fancy stuff isn't my idea of what a garden should be. A garden should be practical, like mine!"

Julian coughed. This was not a good start. "Don't worry, Mr—er?"

"Malcolm, from Number 10."

"Well, Mr—er—Malcolm. We'll go and look at your garden once the meeting is over and you can explain to us what you would like. I'm sure we can come to some agreement."

Linda gave him a sharp nudge with her elbow.

"Don't get all stroppy, Malcolm, before they've started. It'll sort itself out."

"It better had! I'm not losing my veggies and that's that!"

Malcolm subsided into a grumpy heap.

"We just love this one, don't we, Guy, quite divine. A Persian Garden; we already have a gazebo where we sit and have a glass of wine on summer evenings and listen to the birdsong from our tapes. The water running along a culvert in front of the gazebo and the blue tiles lining the sides and along the paths is a wonderful idea." Damian was full of enthusiasm.

"I like these little orange trees in square wooden boxes along the paths," joined in Guy.

"They're all the same and so neat and pleasing; but orange trees, in our climate?"

"Quite possible," said Beatrice, "but it's best to take them in somewhere warmer in the really cold weather, perhaps a conservatory."

"Alas, no; that's something we would really like but can't afford."

"Well, you can always use clipped box or something similar."

"Marvellous! We'll plump for a little piece of Paradise, then."

The two men shared a smile at the prospect.

Julian breathed a sigh of relief. Two satisfied customers apparently.

"So that's where all those birds come from in the evenings," muttered Malcolm.

"Cuckoos in the late summer never sounded right to me."

Damian, who was sitting next to Linda overheard the remark and gave Malcolm a withering look. He had never met his neighbour before as he and Guy kept themselves to themselves to avoid trouble; just as well it would seem as Malcolm looked like a prize fighter with his stocky frame and muscular arms and his shaved head. Not the kind of person they associated with; totally lacking in finesse and a bully as well. The rows which had emanated from next door, which appeared to involve their daughter had not been lost on Damian and Guy. Even the thick walls of the terrace houses had not kept them from hearing what was going on and it was a relief at times to go out to Guy's club in the evenings.

"I have an eight year old daughter who would love a place all of her own in the garden; her own special area," said Millie, who like everyone else was getting tired of hearing Malcolm throwing his weight about. "I don't have much time for gardening so I think this plan for raised beds and gravel paths would suit me. My lawn mower is ancient and I find it heavy to use so

Jan Pollard

getting rid of most of the grass would suit me fine, but I'd like to keep a little bit for Lucy and her pet rabbit which I could cut with shears or a strimmer."

Julian turned to face the speaker. Millie was looking up towards him from her position on the floor cushion where she sat with her arms around her knees. Her slim figure and the curtain of long blonde hair which encircled her heart shaped face made her look younger than her years. Julian was entranced. This project could have possibilities as far as she was concerned. She had an eight year old daughter but apparently there was no man to help her with the garden. He flashed her one of his most winning smiles.

"We'll do all we can to help. Beatrice and I will give thought to your ideas and I will show you our plans as soon as they are ready for your approval. We were hoping that someone would like raised flower beds, so that will be fine." His smile lingered for a while as his eyes caressed her body. She was a peach ready for the picking, maybe.

Millie nodded her assent and smiled shyly, only too aware of his interest in her.

Mike seethed inwardly. He would have to make his move before this Romeo got his hands on her. Millie's husky voice was soft and deep and sexy, and her lips as she spoke were pink and full and eminently kissable. Mike had felt a flame of desire spreading through his limbs as she had spoken. As she lifted her head to speak he had seen her large deep blue eyes and her long eyelashes. It was just as he had imagined in his dreams when he had held her in his arms and felt the breasts he had once seen so briefly in silhouette, and had longed to touch ever since.

His fantasies came to a sudden end as Ruth hissed in his ear.

"What about us, Mike? You have no time for gardening either, so how about this?"

"A Zen garden; I don't know—there's not much in it."

"Suit you, Mike, hardly any maintenance; a garden for contemplation. You do a lot of that!"

Beatrice, hearing the caustic tone in Ruth's voice looked up. This was a woman after her own heart if she was not mistaken.

Whatever the relationship between this couple the woman wore the trousers. Beatrice was interested having no time for men herself and this woman looked like her type. She would soon find out as Zen gardens meant nothing to Julian and she had only added them to the list of suggestions as they were her special interest.

"It's an unusual idea for a garden in an area such as this, but we wanted to make each garden completely different for the programme. I would be delighted to explain the meaning behind it to you at a later date. There's a lot to learn about the simplicity of a Zen garden and how it makes an area of perfect harmony."

"*Harmony with Ruth!*" thought Mike, bitterly, who failed to understand her interest in the idea. It did nothing for him; all that gravel in a dry garden, raked to represent waves.

Ruth was held by the spell the other woman wove. Her eyes sparkled with interest and Beatrice could see a future disciple; an intelligent woman seeking enlightenment, if she had read the signs correctly.

"I look forward to it," said Ruth, quietly.

Mike wondered if his ears were deceiving him. Ruth was showing an interest in their garden. Wonders would never cease.

"I'm sorry we haven't been able to contact the person who seems to live in the last house. Did you have any luck, Mrs Collins?" asked Venus.

"I'm afraid I didn't," answered Linda.

"We live next to that tip," grumbled Malcolm.

"It's a disgrace, that's what it is—a blot on the landscape. I hope you're going to do something about it. If not, I'm not having anything to do with this programme and you might as well know that now."

Ed groaned inwardly. "We intend to, Malcolm, I promise you. We have plans to make the corner garden into a healing garden, full of herbs and scented plants to quieten the spirit and calm the soul, but first we must make contact with the owner or the person who lives there; you must realise that."

Malcolm grunted in reply, peeved by the murmur of laughter which appeared to be directed towards him.

Jan Pollard

"What's in it for us; apart from the publicity?" asked Malcolm, crossly.

"Well, we're allocating two thousand pounds for each garden to cover the cost of the clearance, the plants and everything else you will need. Some of that money will come to you; it will depend on how much you spend on the garden itself and how complicated the design. But with your help and permission to record your viewpoint about the work as it progresses and a little about yourselves, we should be able to produce a really interesting programme over a period of seven weeks. You will benefit in many ways; not least from the illustrated book on the project from which you will receive royalties."

"What will the seventh programme be about? There are only six gardens," asked Guy, out of interest.

"We will invite the public to visit you all on an open day and 'phone in their comments, and maybe award a prize to the most interesting garden. We are still considering that. Are there any more questions?"

"When do you start? I have my potatoes to put in."

"Hopefully, in two weeks time, at the beginning of March, Mr—er—Malcolm; it will be a mess for a few weeks I'm warning you, but the end results should be fantastic, so please be patient."

As the meeting came to an end and people got ready to leave, Venus invited them all to a summer barbecue in their garden when everything was finished. It brought smiles to everyone's face apart from Malcolm who had no time for such foreign ideas.

"I'm sure our William will be pleased to help in Edna's garden, if he can be paid for it," suggested Linda. "He's a big strong boy, like his Dad, and would be glad of the money."

"I'll consider it," said Ed, hoping that William was less aggressive than his father.

Linda beamed at Ed, hopefully, and Malcolm gave her a look of amazement.

"Sometimes Linda, I do believe there's a brain lurking inside that empty head of yours."

Linda smiled. She considered the remark to be a compliment from her husband.

CHAPTER 5

March had 'come in like a lion' as the saying goes, and the gardens of the Close were waterlogged after weeks of rain. Benji was busy grinding pimento in his pestle and mortar creating a hot dish which he had decided to call, 'Fiery Pepper Pot', when there was a thundering knock at the back door. As nobody could reach the back of the houses in the middle of the terrace unless they had climbed over the fence, Benji opened the door with care. A powerfully built man wearing a singlet and dirty jeans stood on the step. Behind him two other men were dismantling the back fences of the properties, opening up a previously unseen vista of the embankment at the side of the railway line.

"Just to let you know, mate, that we are starting to clear the site before the crew begin filming."

"Fine," said Benji, who vaguely remembered that Venus had said something about it as she had got ready to leave while he was still half asleep. Mornings were a slow start for Benji who got home in the early hours from Rowlands and struggled to get up in time to take over the care of his daughter.

He stood on the back step for a few moments to look at the view. The city train rattled along the line, the roofs of the carriages glistening with rain as they passed below the top of the embankment. Beyond the line were row upon row of fences bordering the gardens of suburban houses. Benji missed the back fence already and the privacy it afforded the terrace, but he supposed that Venus and Ed knew what they were doing. The workmen had to get into the back gardens with their rotovators from somewhere, and the top of the embankment was the only point of access. They could use the small gate into Millie's garden, but Edna's passage was too small for anything other than a wheelbarrow. Soon there would be lorries delivering sand and bags of cement, slabs and concrete mixers and skips for all the garden rubbish, parked outside the front windows.

Benji went back to his new recipe and began to prepare the meat to be marinated. It certainly would be a 'Fiery Pepper Pot' by the time he had finished with it—just right for this cold weather. He could imagine Malcolm getting hot under the collar when the workmen started to clear his vegetable patch. Benji chuckled to himself. A right 'Fiery Pepper Pot' that Malcolm was to be sure!

Everyone in the terrace, apart from Number 6, had received a letter to tell them the date when the work was to commence. Ed made sure that the workmen knocked on each door first in case one of the residents had forgotten and got upset, but there was nobody in apart from Benji and Mike.

"We can't raise the person at Number 2. Perhaps you'll let the lady know we're starting to-day," said the man in charge, to Mike.

"Yes, of course. She'll be back soon I expect, she's just taken her little girl to school."

Mike could hardly believe his luck. He had a valid reason to call on Millie and intended to make the most of this opportunity. As soon as he heard her front door shut he smoothed down his hair in the hall mirror, and once satisfied with his appearance, he walked round to Number 2 and knocked. When Millie opened the door and he found himself face to face with her he began to feel nervous. She might not want to know him. "I'm Mike, from next door. You remember me, don't you; from the resident's meeting? Could I have a word, if it's not inconvenient?"

The Hidden Gardens

"Of course—come in."

Millie was surprised to see him. Mike's wife was far from being her favourite person but Mr Fairweather had always seemed friendly enough, waving to them as she took Lucy to school. In fact she had often thought he must have a pretty lonely life working in his little room day after day while his wife was teaching; and what a wife! Still, for all she knew he might love the old harridan. Opposites were often attracted to each other.

Millie ushered him into the kitchen, so different from his own; a real family kitchen, with Lucy's things scattered over the table, the breakfast plates still in the sink and a heap of washing waiting to be put in the machine.

"Would you like a cup of coffee? I often have one after I've left Lucy at school."

"Lovely, thanks." Mike, who had just had a cup of coffee, would have drunk a dozen more if she had offered them; anything to stay with her for a while.

Millie put on the kettle and glanced out of the window.

"Oh! They've started! Doesn't it look different without the back fence? You can see all the other gardens across the embankment."

Mike came to stand beside her, longing to put his arm round her waist as they looked at the view. Strands of her long hair touched his cheek. It smelled fresh, like lemons. Mike was in heaven. He wanted to kiss each strand and found it difficult to restrain himself.

"That's what I came to tell you. The workmen wanted everyone to know they were starting today, and you had gone out."

"Oh, I'd only taken Lucy to school. I know it isn't far but there's the main road to cross and children are so vulnerable these days. I like to take and fetch her myself. It's silly of me I expect. She's old enough to go on her own, but she's all I've got."

"I understand perfectly. I see you most days from my office; taking her and bringing her home."

Millie smiled, and went to make the coffee.

Jan Pollard

"It must be lonely, working on your own all day."

"Yes, it is. I miss the company of the people in my old office but the partnership broke up. It's not having anyone to talk to that's the worst. I find myself talking to myself sometimes; the first signs of madness so they say!"

Mike smiled at her and the smile was returned.

"You must be glad when it's the school holidays and your wife is at home."

There was a silence between them as they sipped their coffee.

"Not really; we don't have much in common."

"Oh, I'm sorry ..."

Millie was at a loss as to how to continue the conversation.

"Don't be sorry. She has her interests and I have mine; the golf club and squash, and I keep busy with work—too busy sometimes. You're fortunate in having a daughter as company. I would have liked children, but Ruth, well, children and Ruth don't agree."

Millie sipped her coffee, thoughtfully, and looked at him over her cup.

"Lucy is in her class."

"I know—I expect she finds it hard sometimes."

Millie put down her cup and spread her hands on the table in a gesture of hopelessness.

"I have a job to get her to go to school these days. She gets so upset."

Millie's eyes filled with tears. Mike was appalled and took her hands in his to comfort her.

"That's awful; it really is. I wish I could do something about it, but I can't. We don't have much to say to one another these days. You should make a complaint to the head teacher." Mike spoke angrily. He felt somehow responsible for the distress his wife had caused this caring young woman who was bringing up her daughter on her own.

"I've tried, but she supports her staff. I get nowhere with her."

Millie removed her hands to get out her handkerchief and blew her nose.

"You're so kind. It seems terrible to be talking to you about this. I've been bottling this up for ages. Please forgive me—it was unforgivable. You won't mention this conversation to Mrs Fairweather, will you? It would only make things worse for Lucy."

"Of course I won't, I wouldn't dream of it; but it might be of some comfort to you to know that Ruth is hoping to move to another job soon, so she could be leaving."

"That's good news as far as Lucy is concerned; but what about you?"

"It's time Ruth and I went our separate ways. Now we have this garden scheme just taking off I can't leave until that is finished anyway. We can't sell a house with a mess in the backyard, although how anyone will find a Zen garden attractive I can't imagine."

Millie looked up at him. She felt easy in his company and he was a really kind man to listen to her troubles. Changing the subject might be a good idea. She had already said too much about his wife and that was inexcusable, but he hadn't seemed to have minded, just the opposite. He had understood which had been amazing.

"You said you wanted a word with me, Mike. What was it about?"

"Did I? Oh, yes, I'd forgotten, how stupid of me." Mike grinned. "What I really wanted to do was to offer you my help with the garden. It's a lot for a woman to do on her own and the Zen garden looks fairly easy to set up and maintain."

"Are you sure you could manage that as well as your work?"

"I'm absolutely sure."

"You really are kind, Mike. I was a bit concerned about the personal involvement. Lucy wants to sow seeds and plant bulbs, bless her, but that's not going to help me much. The money is important, you see. It's a chance to make ends meet. Hairdressing at home doesn't bring in much. I live off the rents from the students but students have such long holidays. I want Lucy to have a good life. I decided to bring her into the world when her father wanted me to have an abortion, so I am responsible for her; you understand don't you. When her father walked out my parents had us here but they are both dead now so it's just Lucy and me."

Mike wished he had been around for her years ago.

"I'm always here; just the other side of the wall, if you ever need any help. You can 'phone me on my mobile. This is my card. Ruth has her own so any call to me will be private; but remember, school holidays aren't a good time to call round. Any other time and you will be more than welcome."

There was a ring at the bell and Mike got up to leave. It was Millie's first hair appointment and she directed the woman into her tiny salon, promising to be with her shortly.

"I'm sorry I have to go now Mike, but come again soon. It's been lovely to talk to you and when the garden gets going I shall be grateful for your help."

"Any time," said Mike as he left, hating to leave her, and longing to kiss her goodbye.

It was a beginning and an unexpected one. She had been friendly towards him which was a good start, but in two weeks time it would be Easter and Ruth would be home for two weeks holiday. He made up his mind to call on her again before then now the ice had been broken and now he had met her, his longing for her had only increased.

Millie found it difficult to sustain a conversation with her client as she washed and blow dried her hair. Her meeting with Mike Fairweather had disturbed her. She had liked him. He had been kind and understanding and was the most gorgeous looking man she had ever met, but nothing took away from the fact that he was married, and married to Lucy's dreaded teacher, which made it worse. Had he told her the truth about his relationship with his wife? Men were only too eager to run down their wives when they wanted an affair, and then to go back to them when it suited them. She had been hurt badly once and was too wise to risk that again, and yet, he had sounded lonely and she knew what his wife was like. She was cruel and unkind to her dear quiet Lucy, so perhaps she was like that to her husband as well. She had been lonely for a long time and an affair would be wonderful with someone like him, but how would Lucy feel if she ever found out? The terrible Mrs Fairweather's husband! It could damage the loving relationship she had with her daughter, and that must never happen. Millie snagged her client's hair with the brush and apologised profusely.

"Aren't you feeling well, dear?" asked the woman. "You're usually so chatty."

"Sorry; I'm fine. Just got something on my mind, that's all"

She took her client's money and helped her into her coat.

"Not a man is it, Millie?"

Millie was shaken by the remark. Was it so obvious!

"Oh no, certainly not. No more men in my life; no way!"

After the woman had gone she began to clean up the basin ready for the next appointment, but she found it impossible to get Mike out of her mind. He had looked as if he could eat her; as if he was already in love with her, and yet how could that be? He had only met her briefly at the residents meeting and yet she had made a great impression on him it would seem. Perhaps they would get to know each other better as the gardens took shape. Millie began to look forward to the beginning of the project with a happy anticipation she had not felt before.

When Guy returned with the shopping he was shattered to find the gazebo at the bottom of the garden had been taken to pieces and placed against the side fence. Damian would be furious when he found out, and get into one of his 'states', and need calming down. Guy dumped the shopping in the kitchen and went to speak to the workmen.

"I say! That's a bit much! We knew about the fence coming down so you could get access, but the gazebo! Nobody told us about that!"

The man in charge came across to speak to Guy. He recognised the voice immediately, it was unmistakable.

"Guy, isn't it? The barman from the club in Pimlico; I'm Gerry. How are ya?"

The wind was taken out of Guy's sails.

"Good Lord! You know me?"

"I'm a member, mate; Gerry Finch. Seen you behind the bar a good many times."

Jan Pollard

"One of us then; pleased to meet you Gerry—*very* pleased to meet you, in fact." Guy shook his hand enthusiastically.

Guy sized him up. He had huge muscular arms and a massive torso. It was cold and wet and yet he only wore a singlet and appeared not to feel the cold. A real butch type and he was in charge of this gang of workmen. What luck!

"How long is your contract here, old love?"

"Six weeks. We do all the hard labour; rotovating, putting down the slabs, laying the turf, making the patios, you name it; we do it."

"Six weeks, lovely. Come in and see me some time, Gerry. I'm here on my own all day, you know, coffee break whenever you fancy it. The others aren't invited."

"Can't resist that now can I? Is this your little nest, or does someone else live here?"

"It belongs to Damian Wentworth. He's my present partner; a lot older than me, but 'any port in a storm,' so to speak. He's out all day running a bookshop in Westminster, so he won't be around."

"Jealous type, is he?"

"A rather sad old queen—but you won't meet him."

"See ya then, Guy." And Gerry left to get on with the job. Guy was well known at the club for his conquests. His present partner had better look out. A change might be in the air.

Guy rang Damian to tell him about the gazebo being removed, and as expected, Damian went off the deep end at the other end of the line. Guy was very conciliatory. Damian would have calmed down by the time he got home and he would cook him his favourite meal of salmon en croûte. His meeting with Gerry Finch would not be mentioned. That would remain Guy's little secret.

When Malcolm arrived home for his tea the whole Close heard the fuss. His potting shed had been removed, and what was even worse, it had been taken away and put in a skip. Admittedly it was in a state of near collapse and let in the rain. Spiders hung in their webs underneath the roof and mice had been known to gnaw their way in through the sides, but Malcolm never noticed such things. It was the place where he sat on fine evenings to smoke a cigarette and contemplate his vegetables unless the birdsong issuing forth from the gazebo next door sent him to the pub for a bit of peace.

Linda never went inside it. She had a phobia about spiders and there were plenty to see inside there. It was Malcolm's place and he was welcome to it. On her return home to cook his tea she was unaware that the potting shed had been removed.

Malcolm looked around for his garden tools and found them all neatly stacked along the fence, plus all his pots and trays and garden netting. Nothing was missing that he could see, but the indignity of having the shed dumped in a skip without a by your leave was too much to bear. Somebody was going to pay for this, and at the moment there was only Linda to take it out on. He roared indoors where Linda was cooking a sirloin steak for his tea, and slammed the back door. "Why didn't you stop them from taking down my shed, you silly cow?"

"I wasn't here when they took it down, Malcolm, and I'd remind you to mind your manners. I was at the launderette all day and when I got home the men and the shed had gone."

"What bloody cheek! I knew I shouldn't have agreed to this barmy idea. I'm going round to see that Nigerian woman right now. She's at the back of this."

"She's Jamaican, not Nigerian, Malcolm, and she's got a very big husband, don't forget," said Linda, patiently, taking the steak out of the frying pan and putting it to warm. She had no idea when Malcolm would eat it now. He would probably go down the pub for a few drinks and to air his grievances once he had finished with Venus. Linda felt sorry. Venus was a decent sort and Linda had hoped to get a patio out of the deal, but knowing Malcolm, he would probably upset everyone so nothing got done.

Malcolm was so long coming back that Linda gave the steak to William when he came in. William enjoyed the rare treat and ate it quickly in case his father returned to claim it, and disappeared soon afterwards to meet up with his mates.

By the time Malcolm returned his mood had changed. Benji had met him at the door with a smile big enough to calm a raging bull and had invited him in. He put off his return to Rowlands that evening until Malcolm had calmed down. A glass of rum had also helped to take the heat out of the situation. Venus apologised for the removal of the potting shed and offered him one twice the size in return, with a greenhouse on the side. Malcolm was placated and returned to his steak to find that William had eaten it and the row blew up all over again. Eventually Malcolm decided to eat at the pub to everyone's relief and peace was restored to the Close.

Upstairs, in her buttercup yellow bedroom, Alice Collins put the last of her belongings into a holdall and wrote a note to her mother. She had decided to leave home now, for ever. Her father got everyone down and she was thoroughly sick of life in the same house.

Another life beckoned; a life with her lover in Cardiff, where he had rented a flat for them and been appointed as head of science at the local comprehensive. She would be sixteen next week and her father no longer had any rights over her as a parent. She had a ticket in her purse to Cardiff and only had to get to the Victoria coach station to be on her way to what she imagined would be everlasting happiness. She would be a mother herself in six months' time, a fact which she had kept to herself in case it had affected the suitability of her lover to take a new post. She had been underage when they had started their clandestine affair and she had sworn to everyone that no sex had been involved for his sake. He was a domineering individual, rather like her father, but Alice was unable to see how that had been part of the attraction. He told her that he loved her and her father never said things like that to anyone, so Linda had been swept away with the whole business of a secret love affair with such an important man. The fact that he was very soon to discover that he had made her pregnant, when he already had a wife and three children, which he had omitted to tell her, was yet to come.

Linda had gone out to play bingo and forget her troubles when her daughter, Alice, left her note on the kitchen table. There was no address and no mention of the baby. Just to say

The Hidden Gardens

she had gone for good. Not even finishing with love and kisses to her mother, and for Linda that was the cruellest blow of all.

Edna was sitting on her usual seat near the park gate. She had put down a sheet of newspaper on the bench which she had found in the adjoining waste bin, as the seat was still wet from the last shower of rain. It was time to go as the park was locked at six each evening, and it was getting cold. She waited for the park keeper to speak to her as he did every evening when he locked up.

"Come on, Missus. Haven't you got a home to go to?"

He said the same thing every time, which Edna found comforting. Hardly anyone ever spoke to her and usually avoided sitting next to her, as she sat clutching her large canvas bag, and feeding the sparrows and the ducks.

Edna would get to her feet and shuffle off across the road to Number 12, where she would light the oil stove and fill the old tin kettle from the water butt, to make some tea. This evening things looked a bit different. In front of the house stood a skip filled with old pieces of wood, a shopping trolley, two old dustbins, part of a bicycle and an ancient pram. Edna stood for some time looking at them. The pram seemed familiar but she had no idea where she had seen it before.

Once indoors she noticed that there seemed to be more light than usual coming through the dirty kitchen window. Someone had been clearing her garden. Edna was amazed and looked outside. Now she remembered where she had seen the pram before. It had come from her garden. She had no use for it, so it might as well stay out in the front. Perhaps someone else would like it, and if so, they might as well have it. A long time ago there had been a baby in it. Her mind cleared slightly and she remembered a chubby, laughing child, holding out its hands to her, and she had picked it up and brought it indoors. Then her memory faded and the baby was no more. The kettle was boiling and remembering how to make the tea took up all her attention.

The following day Edna went to the park as usual, but this was not going to be a day like any other day. She went to the ladies toilet as she usually did on her arrival, there not being any water in her own house for flushing a toilet or for washing purposes, and then she heard a man's voice shouting to everyone to clear the area. Once she had collected herself together Edna peered round the door to see the park keeper locking the gates. It was much too early for that surely; she had only just arrived. People were running in all directions and there were police everywhere in Park Close. Then there was silence for a while and Edna crept closer to the gate to see what was happening. Suddenly two army trucks drove up to the door of Number 12 and soldiers jumped out. Edna waited no longer. She had seen enough. They had come for her at last.

She began to weep with fright and hid herself amongst the dusty bushes beside the railings. Her husband Franz had never come home for a long time now. They must have tortured him to find out where she lived and now she would be put in a concentration camp like all her other relatives and never be heard of again.

Park Close seemed deserted. One of the army trucks moved away but the other one was still parked outside her front door. Edna stayed very still. Nobody came looking for her which was what she had expected. It was very strange. Where were all the people who lived in the Close? There was no sign of anyone; not even a policeman.

A few hours passed by and she heard some soldiers talking to one another. Something was lifted into the truck and driven away. After a while she heard people's voices and peered out of her hiding place to see Linda talking to the coloured lady with the baby and her husband. Other people who lived at the end of the Close came to talk to them too and then went inside their houses. So nobody else had been taken away. Edna considered it was safe to go home but when she got to the gate it was still locked.

When it began to get dark Edna settled herself down on her usual seat on a pad of newspaper she had found in the bin beside her and cushioned her head on her large carrier bag which was fairly soft with all the paper and bread she kept inside it. The ducks had gone to sleep for the night with their heads tucked under their wings. Edna found some comfort in looking at their still forms and eventually she too fell asleep.

In the morning, once the gate was unlocked she set off for home. Linda, who was just setting off for the launderette after a wretched night of weeping over her daughter's note, saw Edna crossing the road.

"Where were you yesterday, Edna? Venus looked for you everywhere but you were nowhere to be found. You missed all the fun."

"Fun," said Edna, bemused. "I saw the soldiers."

"Well, it wasn't really fun," Linda could see she was puzzled, "more of a nuisance really. We all had to go the Church Hall while they defused the bomb in your backyard."

"A bomb in my backyard!" Edna was aghast. "Has the war started again? I saw the soldiers come to take me away."

"Goodness me no; they hadn't come for you, Edna. Why on earth would they do that? They defused the bomb and then they took it away to blow it up somewhere else."

"A bomb, they took the bomb away?"

"It's gone now, Edna, and it's safe for us all to go home, but it's a miracle we weren't all blown to bits. The men who cleared your garden found it, and what a good job they did. Look, I've got a few minutes. I'll show you where it was so you don't fall into the hole." Linda, who was glad to forget her own troubles for a minute led Edna round to the back of the garden where a large crater was evident, filling up most of her backyard. Edna peered down into the depths.

"Whatever you do, Edna, don't fall in there. I shouldn't go into the backyard until the men have filled it in if I was you."

"What about my kettle?"

Linda failed to understand the question. "What kettle, Edna?"

"The kettle I boil for my tea."

"Don't you keep that indoors? Surely that wasn't in your backyard?"

"No," Edna was beginning to get flustered, "the water for my tea—out of there." She pointed to the water butt.

"But haven't you got a tap inside, Edna?"

"No, it doesn't work. I fill it there."

Linda was shocked; things were worse than anyone had imagined.

"Well, you give me your kettle and I'll fill it up for you. Perhaps tomorrow the hole will have been filled in and then it will be safe to go outside."

Edna pushed open her front door and brought out her rusty kettle and Linda filled it for her. "You only have to ask," she said, kindly, "any time."

Linda related this incident to Malcolm while he ate his tea.

"She was scared of the soldiers, Malcolm. It was weird."

Malcolm grinned. "Perhaps she'd absconded from the forces during the war; Edna a deserter. Too old for them to bother about her now, I should think." He laughed at what he considered was a joke.

"No, Malcolm; it was something far worse than that; it must have been."

"She was rambling, that's all. You know Edna; she doesn't know one day from the other."

Linda shrugged and made no reply. There was something funny about it just the same.

CHAPTER 6

Before Easter arrived the gardens in the Close had been cleared of everything apart from a few mature trees which it was considered would enhance rather than detract from the makeover. Mike had visited Millie twice for coffee and a chat when she had time to spare from her usual hairdressing appointments, once after ringing her to suggest it and once when she had asked him. They seemed to have such a lot in common and Mike gave her advice on her banking arrangements. It was developing into a close friendship but not as close as Mike would have liked. Millie was worried about Lucy's reaction if she had known that her mother was getting friendly with Mr Fairweather and that held her back. It was becoming obvious that Mike wanted it to be a loving relationship. He sent her flowers and brought her chocolates and kissed her gently on the cheek each time he left. He was loving and kind and very considerate and lonely like herself but there was always this worry at the back of her mind that stopped her from flinging her arms round him and telling him how much he meant to her. Perhaps if his wife moved on to this better position, which was her one great hope, and Lucy had another teacher, then they could become lovers and maybe live together. Until that happened Millie kept him at arm's length although he had awakened in her the urge to sleep with him. She so longed to be wanted and desired in that way again and she knew that was Mike's greatest wish as well but she was afraid to commit herself. All hell would be let loose if his wife found out and Lucy would suffer the most.

And then Julian Goodwood came to call and Millie's world turned upside down. On the last day of term a smart sports car drew up outside Number 2 and Julian stepped out and opened the boot. Mike watched from his office window as he took out what appeared to be a garden statue of a young girl sitting reading on a pillar of stone. This he deposited on Millie's doorstep, and then returned for a roll of paper and a large gold wrapped Easter egg. Mike was annoyed. He was making headway with Millie and wanted no other men on the scene. He had seen Julian looking her over at the resident's meeting and he had a good idea as to what he had come for, and Millie was alone in the house. Mike wondered if Julian had arranged this meeting as there were no ladies that morning coming to have their hair appointments as usual.

Millie came to the door, all smiles, as she accepted the Easter egg and was obviously delighted when Julian picked up the statue to show her. The door closed on them and Mike was plunged into gloom. He presumed the roll of paper was the new plan for the garden which he had promised her at the meeting, so they would be bending over it together as he described the garden to her. Perhaps her long blonde hair was touching his cheek, as it had touched his once. Mike was consumed with jealousy and considered ringing her on some pretext but common sense decreed that would not be a wise move.

It was a beautiful spring morning and the daffodils were out in the park opposite his window. Mike could find no pleasure in looking at them. He went downstairs to make himself a sandwich for lunch and then found he had no appetite. Suddenly he heard them talking in the garden and opened the back door. They were at the end of the garden where Julian was describing a rose covered trellis with an archway in the centre, leading to a secret garden for Lucy.

"Of course it will be very small," he was explaining, "but the kind of garden she can make into her very own. We'll plant three silver birch trees in the corner and the statue can stand underneath. There can be a willow arbour in the opposite corner which she can help make, weaving the withes in and out round the sides. It'll grow denser every year and become her private space. We'll put a seat inside and if she would like it, a stone bird bath in the centre of her garden so she can enjoy watching the birds as they come to drink."

"You're wonderful to have thought of this, Julian. It's just what Lucy would love."

So he had come to discuss the garden thought Mike and he went back to his office to get on with some work. Listening to Julian was the last thing he wanted to do.

"And what would her beautiful mother love?" asked Julian, stroking Millie's cheek with his finger. "Tell me and all her wishes will be granted." His eyes creased with laughter and his lips parted slightly to show his perfect teeth. He bent towards her and his lips brushed her cheek. He placed a thumb under her chin and lifted her face towards him.

"Well, Millie? You haven't answered my question."

Millie swallowed. He had no interest whatsoever in any plans she might have for the garden. He had come for a sexual encounter and for that alone, and she was taken aback by his effrontery. He had presumed too much.

"The rabbit—," she managed to say, moving away from him.

Julian laughed as if it was a joke she was playing on him. "What rabbit? Where is it? Am I treading on it, or something?"

"Of course not; it's just that Lucy will want somewhere to put her rabbit in her garden, and some grass for it to run about in, and a border for her bulbs and seeds—." Millie gabbled on, the words came tumbling out for Julian had disturbed her deeply and she found herself trembling. She had kept men at bay, and that included Mike to whom she felt sexually attracted, since Lucy's father had left her. She mistrusted them apart from Mike, whom she had learned to care about, because he was kind and decent and had taken their friendship gently, but this man had awoken a strong sexual urge in her which she felt unable to control. He was so beautiful, with his tanned skin and handsome looks and the way he touched her, which gave her goose pimples.

He drew her towards him in a close embrace and kissed her lips, gently at first, until she no longer pulled away and kissed him back despite herself. Her knees turned to jelly and she was consumed with the need to make passionate love. Her mouth parted and she found herself begging him to make love to her.

"I want you, Millie. I've wanted you since I first saw you, and you want me, don't you? Come on; let's go indoors. There's no privacy here and I can't wait."

Millie felt as if her world had exploded around her as she took his hand and pulled him inside and shut the back door. She needed him too, it had been such a long time, and she was finding it increasingly impossible to keep her feelings in check now she had got to know Mike but for Lucy's sake she had to wait for the right time so there was no danger of Lucy suffering from the relationship. Having sex with this stranger meant there were no restrictions. She would probably never see him again and nobody need ever know.

Millie tore off her clothes and they stumbled into the front room and rolled together naked on the rug in front of the gas fire. Julian was a practised lover and licked and nuzzled her until there was no time left for foreplay as Millie found herself reaching heights of ecstasy she had never before experienced. He was an insatiable lover and their love making went on for most of the afternoon until Millie suddenly remembered that Lucy would be waiting for her, and came down to earth. Pulling away from him she dressed quickly explaining as she did so that she had to collect her daughter and had no idea how late it was getting.

"Little Millie Mouse you *are* a surprise," said Julian, as he got dressed. "What shall I give you for such an enjoyable afternoon? How about a pergola, full of exotic garden furniture? Mind you, a conservatory might be on the cards if you continue to be so obliging and we make it a regular date. What say you?"

There was a hint of a sneer on his smiling face as he kissed her cheek and left. He had achieved what he had come for and

The Hidden Gardens

there might be even more if she was willing, but she had given him no answer as she hurried to put on her clothes.

Mike watched him roar away in his sports car. Julian had been with Millie for most of the afternoon and Mike guessed there had been more to it than a conversation about the garden. Perhaps Ruth had been right about her all along, but he felt he knew her better than that. For him she was a perfect woman; his ideal.

Millie came out and locked the front door and hurried up the road. She gave no indication that she had seen Mike's wave which he found surprising as it was usual for her always to acknowledge him these days since they had become friends. Mike felt hurt.

Something had happened to change things. Surely she hadn't fallen for that lady's man; not Millie!

Millie was in a daze. She felt as if she had come alive again. Julian had shown her the joys of sex in ways she had never thought possible, and she had to admit to herself that she had enjoyed the experience after all her years of abstention. The powerful animal magnetism between them had opened up a new world and she felt an enormous sense of release, although for the man himself she felt nothing. He had simply used her for his own self gratification. In fact she despised him, trying to buy her services with promises of expensive additions to the garden, as if she was a common prostitute, as he had left. She had behaved in a wild, abandoned way which now she thought about it, embarrassed her, and she hoped he would keep his distance from now on. He was a dangerous man with a power over women which she had found impossible to resist. Just a touch on her cheek and a kiss on her lips had been enough to fire her emotions and to turn her into a willing participant in his sexual romps. The experience made her realise how much she had missed all these years, nursing a deep resentment towards men for the hurt she had suffered in the past, while she had struggled to be a good mother to Lucy.

As she returned home with Lucy she glanced up at Mike's office window, but Mike had gone. If only he could resolve his marital situation things could be good between them. She had made Lucy an excuse to keep him from becoming too close to her and perhaps that had been a mistake. Mike genuinely loved her, his eyes spoke volumes every time he looked at her, the least she could have done was to show him that she cared for him too, but she had been afraid to make her feelings too obvious. In September Lucy would be in another class with another teacher and then she would show him how she felt. Sex was meaningless without love, but with Mike it would be wonderful.

Mike had gone downstairs to get his golf clubs. He would go to the club and smack a few balls around the course to ease the pain he felt. He ached physically for Millie in every way, and she must have realised how much he had longed to touch her and feel her kisses on his lips. She never objected to the chaste kiss he planted on her cheek each time they parted, but she made it clear that he was just a dear friend, and Mike was not one to overstep the mark. He would worship her from afar until the time was right, if it would ever be right now. She had spent hours with that sex obsessed Julian who cared nothing for her and it angered him deeply. He hit the ball so hard it missed the green and landed in a bunker. Mike wished it had been Julian Goodwood's head!

When Mike returned home from the golf club he was in a foul mood. Nothing had gone right and his score was a disgrace to any self respecting golfer. He threw his clubs down in the hall and went towards the stairs. He still had some work to finish which he should have done that afternoon but had found it impossible to concentrate. As he ascended the stairs he heard a voice he didn't recognise and then Ruth's delighted reply.

"Wonderful! Just wonderful! I'll look through them all during the holiday and decide what I like best; then perhaps you'll come back and give me your expert advice Beatrice. I shall look forward to that."

Beatrice Thorn was smiling as she was ushered to the door. She reminded Mike of a horsey type of woman, with her short cropped dark hair, her thick tweed jacket and large practical brogues. There was nothing feminine about her, apart from her large bust.

"It will be my pleasure, my dear Ruth. I look forward to it." Even her voice was deep and masculine, and Mike noticed she had the beginnings of a slight moustache on her top lip.

"Well, what did Beatrice Thorn come for?" asked Mike, from the top of the stairs.

"Oh, there you are, Mike. I wish you'd been here when she came. It was about the garden. She's left all these books on Japanese gardens for us to look at. We're expected to choose which kind we'd like."

"I'll look at them later. I've got a bit of work to finish; didn't feel like it this afternoon, so I went to the Golf Club."

"You don't know what a days work is like these days, skiving off when you feel like it. I wish I could do that."

Mike went back upstairs to finish what he was doing and Ruth went back to her books, making notes as she went and putting markers in the illustrations which attracted her.

Later that evening they looked at them together and Ruth explained what was needed to create such a garden.

"We'll have a stream winding through the garden, running over white gravel to lighten the effect of the moving water, and ending in a pond. That would look lovely. We could put one of those little bridges across the end of the pond, leading to a teahouse tucked away in the corner. What do you think?"

"A teahouse! For heavens sake, Ruth! Isn't the kitchen a suitable enough place for making the tea?"

"It's traditional, that's all. We can use it as a summer house; for sitting in."

"What an odd idea."

"You would think that, Mike. You have no imagination."

"Not that sort, I haven't."

"The idea is to create the perfect harmony of yin and yang. It's a celebration of nature; pure simplicity."

"And what's that may I ask; this yin and yang thing."

Ruth sighed. "It's perfectly easy to understand. Yin is the cold aspect of nature and yang is the opposite. Water and land;

stones, conifers and bamboos for example, and the water running through; the stream is the yin part of it."

"I thought I was supposed to rake gravel when I did the gardening, rather than weed anything; so you could meditate on life in general."

"I don't know about that yet. I think I'd rather have a tea garden now after looking at these pictures. Anyway Beatrice is coming to plan it all. She knows all about Japanese gardens. They're her hobby."

The idea of working on this strange garden with Beatrice Thorn giving him his orders held no appeal for Mike. Still, it would keep Ruth out of his hair for a while, or so he hoped.

"Look at this picture, Mike! See all these stones. It says they contain their own spirits. Isn't that extraordinary! They have to be placed naturally; a tall stone, an arching stone, a recumbent stone and horizontal stones—amazing!"

Mike looked at the picture. Apparently they were to grow stones now rather than plants. Well, that suited him; no weeding.

"No plants, then?" he asked, hopefully.

"Of course there'll be *some* plants, but not many. We could have a cut leaf maple and a Japanese flowering cherry, and azaleas, carefully placed to go in the scheme of things, and a stand of bamboo and grasses. There has to be space apparently—."

"Of course," said Mike, with a hint of sarcasm in his voice. "Space in our back garden, that's a laugh! Look at these pictures, Ruth. There are masses of space where these gardens have been made. Some of them are hundreds of years old. How do you expect to make something like this in our garden? It's impossible."

"What's got into you, Mike? You're as cross as two sticks. Has something upset you today?"

Mike shrugged. "To tell you the truth, I'm not really interested in this bright idea of yours. The only part I like is the pond, with the water lilies and the goldfish and perhaps the quaint little bridge with the stone lanterns at each end. I'll go along with that bit, but don't ask me about the rest."

The Hidden Gardens

"I'll do it myself, then," snapped, Ruth. "Beatrice will help me. She understands me, which is more than you do!"

Mike turned on the television to watch Tiger Woods playing in one of his old tournaments while Ruth continued to turn the pages of her books.

Mike found it hard to concentrate on the match. The thought of what Millie might have been up to that afternoon was driving him mad.

CHAPTER 7

Marking out the gardens began just before Easter. There was to be a break for a week as the television crew would be on holiday, and then work would begin in earnest.

Venus and Ed, the film crew and Beatrice and Julian all arrived together in Edna's garden the intention being to work along the terrace, ending at Number 2, with Julian hoping that afterwards he would be able to spend some time in further dalliance with Millie. The residents had all been told of the plan. A few had replied but most had not bothered to answer. Malcolm, who wanted a say in what was happening to his garden had taken a day off to keep an eye on the proceedings.

Edna was nowhere to be seen for which Venus was grateful, in case she made some objection to them being there. The crew began filming as Julian, using his white marker followed his plan, while Beatrice measured out the areas in which herbs and plants were to be grown. A vertical gravel path, symbolizing masculinity, crossed a horizontal path to represent femininity, in the centre of the garden. A circle surrounded them, and this in its turn was surrounded by a square, leaving four small triangles in the corners for planting.

Julian explained as he went along so the viewers would understand this ancient design for a healing garden.

The Hidden Gardens

"The circle represents heaven, and the square is the earth. The triangles are the four elements from which everything else is derived; earth, water, air and fire. There will be a pool of water in the centre to create a calm stillness in the garden."

Ed was most impressed. Julian, for all his fancy ways knew his job and he was glad he had asked him to take part. Venus took notes, hoping that marking out the other gardens in the Close would go as well as this one, but she was wrong. Malcolm's garden was next and Malcolm was waiting for them.

The group moved on to Number 10 and Ed saw, to his horror, that Malcolm had already dug over the entire top of his garden and planted his early potatoes.

"This wasn't in the plan," objected Ed.

"Maybe not, but it was in *my* plan," said Malcolm, nastily. "They're bloody well in and that's where they're staying."

The conversation was being recorded. "Cut!" shouted Ed, who felt things were not going to form and this part of the programme might have to be scrapped.

There was a hasty discussion between everybody apart from Malcolm, and for the sake of peace it was decided to leave the potatoes undisturbed. Filming started again.

"If we leave this as the top plot," began Julian, in a reasonable tone of voice, "we can have three large plots on either side of a grass path, with paths in between, and a long grass path encompassing the whole garden. It will mean six plots for vegetables instead of eight as I had intended, but it won't really make much difference to the scheme of things."

Malcolm looked triumphant. He had won the first round and was ready for the second.

"I don't want grass paths between my vegetables," he objected. "Grass seeds if it's left and I can't spare the time to keep cutting it, or to weed grass growing between my carrots and onions."

"Of course not," agreed Julian, patiently, "but I had intended the plots to be edged in wood, or anything else you might prefer."

Malcolm was appeased. "*Anything* else I might prefer?"

"Yes, of course, Mr. Collins. It's up to you. We do take into consideration people's feelings on the matter. It's your garden after all."

Beatrice walked across to the new potting shed and the greenhouse, which was stacked waiting for construction.

"I'm sure you're pleased with your new greenhouse, Mr. Collins. We should be able to show you using it in a later programme."

"I shall be more pleased when it's been put together," grumbled Malcolm. "I hope that won't be much longer. I need to plant my tomatoes in there."

"Of course, and I shall be happy to give you tips about using your greenhouse to the best advantage."

Malcolm nearly choked. This woman telling him what to do with his greenhouse made him see red.

"You bloody well won't," he shouted.

Ed waved his arms furiously. "Cut!" he yelled.

There was another hasty discussion between Ed and the presenters.

"His wife wanted an area for her flowers; growing in containers, near the house," said Venus, who was trying to take the heat out of the situation.

"I've taken that into consideration," said Julian. "But he'll have to be told."

"I'll tell him," offered Beatrice. "He doesn't bother me. I've had worse than him to deal with."

She marched across to Malcolm and looked him straight in the eye. No messing around where Beatrice was concerned.

"I'd like to show you what Mr Goodwood has planned for a small area near the house. It won't affect your vegetable garden in any way; in fact it will add to it. Come along. I'll show you what I mean."

Malcolm who wanted to know what this was all about, followed, with the film crew in tow and the cameras rolling.

"This small area here is for plants in pots; flowers for your wife to look after, and maybe strawberries in containers, or outside tomatoes."

"Linda! Look after plants! You don't know what you're talking about. Linda knows bloody well nothing about gardening."

"Well then, you could look after them yourself, Mr. Collins."

"I won't have time with the rest of the garden."

Beatrice was beginning to lose patience with him when the back door opened and Linda appeared. She was wearing a pair of pink trousers which were two sizes too small for her and clung to her figure as if they were about to split at any moment. The buttons on her blouse scarcely met, leaving wide gaps between them and her hair looked a mess. Her face was blotched with crying. The group looked accusingly at Malcolm as if he might be the cause of her distress, but Malcolm had done nothing; just the opposite, he had left her alone to wallow in her misery since their Alice had left, without saying where she was going. Linda had taken it personally. She had loved Alice very much, trying to make up for Malcolm's indifference as a father.

"I really would like a little bit of garden for myself, Malcolm, and I *will* look after it. It would be somewhere for me to sit when it's a nice day, and I'd keep it watered; I promise. You wouldn't have to do anything."

"And so you shall have a garden," said Beatrice, in a sugary tone of voice, as if she was a fairy godmother handing out gifts, except that she looked nothing like the part. "I shall help you to choose the plants for it. You can have easy things to grow, like pelargoniums or begonias; lots of wonderful colours there."

"How about one of those tropical umbrellas to sit under and a teak garden seat," suggested Julian, whose ideas were usually expensive ones.

Malcolm objected strongly. "I need all the money for my garden, not nonsense like that"

Beatrice pointed to the greenhouse. "Well, we could of course exchange this for a cheaper model Mr. Collins, and then you would have more money to spend on the things you want. How does that sound to you?"

"You're not removing that. That stays!!" shouted Malcolm, who was beginning to feel that they were ganging up on him and he was losing out.

"Right, enough said, eh, Mr. Collins? The small patio for your wife will remain. Come along, Julian. We have a lot to do this morning so let's get on with it."

Malcolm had had enough. He stomped off indoors, slammed the front door and went to the pub. Linda, feeling more cheerful, went into the kitchen to make them some tea, to show her gratitude.

The work was completed without any further interruptions and everyone moved on to Number 8.

Guy, unlike Malcolm, was no trouble. He watched as the measuring and marking was carried out and Julian gave his commentary to the cameras, describing the position of the channels for the water. A simple fountain would eventually stand at the top end if things went to plan. Guy could see how beautiful it would be once the gazebo had been replaced. The ancient Persians certainly knew a thing or two about designing gardens. Sadly he would not be here to enjoy it. Two years were the length of time he usually spent with one partner. He became bored after that and needed new diversions and Gerry had come along just at the right time.

Gerry was so different from Damian. He was lively and full of fun and they got along splendidly in every respect. He was tired of Damian and cooking and cleaning and shopping for him. Damian was a lot older and had needed someone to depend on, and Guy had been happy to oblige at the time, especially as he was looking for somewhere to live. Damian suited him. He had found Damian's overwhelming affection flattering at first but life had moved on and he had found someone else.

Gerry took jobs to suit him and then travelled abroad to exotic places where he knew he could find companionship with people of the same persuasion. He seemed to enjoy life enormously and made Guy feel as if he was stuck in a rut. He found Gerry a job behind the bar in the Gay Club and they ran it together. Damian came there occasionally and had met Gerry, but he had no idea of the relationship between the two men, or that Gerry visited Guy daily in his own house, when working on the garden project. He would have been mortified had he discovered that Guy had taken another lover.

There was a distinct coolness about their relationship these days which Damian put down to growing older together and the sameness of daily life. Perhaps if he sold some of his mother's antiques and bought a car, things would improve. Guy would love a car; he might even give it to him, so he could use it as he pleased. The thought cheered Damian immensely. He would do anything to buy back Guy's waning affection.

At Number 6, Venus and Benji had decided on a garden full of colour, with red and orange and purple flowers growing in wild profusion amongst the borders. A large barbecue area was to be sited in the middle of the garden on a raised decking, with an area for sitting and eating. Venus was looking forward to entertaining outside on warm summer evenings while Benji cooked up his recipes for their guests.

A play area was measured outside the French windows so Scrumpi could be seen from the kitchen area as she played. Benji's daily duties would then be made much easier as he worked on writing his recipe books. This was fairly easy to set out and Venus and Benji joined in with the commentary this time, making it a free advertisement for Benji's cookery books, which Ed had allowed as the personal interests of the residents were to be an integral part of the programme.

Beatrice took over at Number 4. She had been to talk to Ruth about her ideas, after her visit to leave the books, and knew exactly what was needed. The order for the teahouse had been placed and there was only the position to be marked where it would stand, with the winding stream through the garden, ending at the pond. Everything else would come together once the stones arrived.

Ruth was at home as the school holidays had begun, and she came out to talk to Beatrice on camera about her enthusiasm for the Japanese garden. Ed was pleased. This would make for good viewing. The whole project was an original idea and he blessed Venus for thinking it up. There had been makeovers before but nothing quite like this with the owners actively involved wherever possible.

Mike stayed away. He failed to understand why Ruth, who never found anything right about anybody or anything, had become so friendly with Beatrice Thorn, and went along with all her crazy ideas about their garden without making any objections. She seemed to have blossomed since the idea took shape, and was a much happier person these days.

Eventually they arrived at house Number 2, the last in the row. It had taken hours and Julian was getting restless. He gave a brief commentary about Lucy's secret garden and then made Beatrice cross as he hustled her along to measure up the four large raised flower beds which he had planned for the rest of the garden. He marked out a small pergola to be attached to the back of the house, although this had not been discussed when he had called on Millie before. Their minds had been on other things then, but he would tell her about it when he saw her this time. She had answered the general letter to say it would be convenient for the film crew to come that day while the garden was being marked out, so he took that to mean that she would be there for him too.

Julian, who had decided he would spend the afternoon with Millie, stayed behind and knocked on her back door. He had explained to the others that he had decided to add a pergola to the back of the house for climbing plants and needed to discuss this addition with Millie which gave him the perfect excuse to call on her alone. He had expected Millie to open it, all smiles at seeing him again but Millie, who knew he was there, sent Lucy instead. Julian was taken aback, not knowing anything about the dates of school holidays, and not expecting Lucy to be at home.

"Mum says she can't come to the door because she's busy with a client, and she's expecting someone else very soon," said Lucy, sweetly.

Julian was speechless. He never had dealings with prostitutes on principle, caring as he did about his own health and the body beautiful. So Millie took clients and was brazen enough to send her young daughter to the door to tell him she was busy plying her trade!

He was horrified and found it hard to believe. She must have pretended she knew so little about sex play the day he had spent with her, when it had been such fun teaching her all the different positions. She must have had him on; she'd known about it all the time.

Julian hurried through the side gate, got into his car without looking back, and sped away, vowing never to return.

Beatrice went round next door to lunch with the Fairweathers once the work was finished. Ruth had invited her while the filming was taking place, and had put a frozen shepherd's pie into the microwave to cook.

"Shepherd's pie, my dear; my favourite!" exclaimed Beatrice, who was starving.

Ruth was pleased and dished her up a large portion. Mike found he only had half as much on his plate, which nobody seemed to notice.

"I'll be glad to see the back of that Julian Goodwood," said Beatrice, as she ate rapidly

"He hustled me around as we were marking out your neighbour's garden, and couldn't wait for us to finish and leave. Mind you, it *was* lunch time and we started very early."

"Perhaps he had another appointment," ventured Mike, who hoped it was with someone other than Millie.

"No doubt; I heard him roar away in that expensive car of his not long afterwards. He's a good garden designer, there's no doubt about that, but the man's a pest to work with, posturing about in front of the cameras as if he's a film star. He thinks no end of himself. I really can't stand him."

Mike would agree with that. "Has he anything else to do with the programme?"

"Not much. He just sees that the planting agrees with his over all design when I have finished my part, that's all. If he doesn't like it, that's too bad. I'm not replacing anything to please *him!*"

"Of course not," said Ruth, in full agreement with her friend.

Mike felt a great sense of relief. Hopefully they had seen the back of Julian Goodwood for a few weeks.

CHAPTER 8

Saturday was a special day for Venus. It was the day when she could spend some quality time with Scrumpi, and the day when Benji had a chance to sleep in late. Friday night at Rowlands was exhausting and Saturdays were even worse. Becoming famous through the 'Cook it my Way,' programme and the follow up recipe books had meant more and more pressure. His salary at Rowlands had gone up by leaps and bounds but there had been a price to pay for fame. Benji had decided that one day he would take his family back to Jamaica, the home of his ancestors and open his own restaurant there. Jamaica was a tourist hotspot these days and it would feel good to be his own boss. It was a dream he shared with Venus, when the time was right and she wanted to move on.

On Saturdays, Venus and Scrumpi visited the launderette and while the clothes were washing they went shopping along the parade. Linda had become very chatty now she had got to know Venus through the garden scheme, and kept Scrumpi amused while Venus loaded the clothes into the machine. It was through this contact that Venus had learned more about Linda and her family troubles. Linda needed someone to confide in and Venus was patient enough to listen to her, and to hear all about her daughter's affair with the science master and Alice's departure from home which had caused Linda such grief.

"She went all moody while that was going on; I could never speak to her, and yet she'd been such a lovely baby, just like yours. I really hated that man—he was old enough to be her father. We were the last people to hear about it, you know. Malcolm went berserk and that didn't help."

"Terrible for you," said Venus sympathetically, imagining the horror of Malcolm going berserk.

"Was he asked to leave?"

"I don't know about that but he left anyway, to take another job. Good riddance to bad rubbish. She was under the age of consent you see, but she swore she had never had sex with him, although all her friends knew what was going on. She thought she was being clever I suppose. You know what girls are like these days. I wasn't a good girl myself with boys, but they were boys, not old men, and now she's gone. God knows where."

Venus felt for her. If Scrumpi left home like that when she was a teenager Venus knew it would feel like the end of the world.

"Perhaps she'll get in touch one day."

"Perhaps," said Linda, sounding doubtful at the prospect of that happening.

This conversation hardly altered every time Venus visited the launderette. Linda had to get it out of her system and Venus listened patiently, hoping that it helped.

One Saturday morning as Venus was posting off a packet of recipes to Benji's publisher she saw Edna in the queue beside her. Edna had taken two pension books out of her large bag and was handing them over the counter to the clerk. There was no quibble about them as the girl paid out the money and pushed it across to Edna. Venus was mystified. It seemed unlikely that Edna would collect a pension for anyone else. They must both belong to her, or perhaps someone else lived in Number 12; someone who never came out. Just seeing Edna in the post office was amazing enough and yet she appeared to know what she was doing.

Once she had posted Benji's packet Venus hurried along to catch up with Edna who was going in the direction of the park and followed discreetly behind. Edna sat on an empty seat by the pond and Venus sat down beside her and watched as Edna fed the ducks with some stale bread she took from her bag. Scrumpi loved it and waved her chubby arms at the ducks as they waddled round her pushchair. Her happy laughter attracted Edna who turned to look at the child. Her face creased into a smile and she held out a piece of bread for Scrumpi to throw, which she promptly put into her mouth. Venus removed it hastily before Scrumpi had time to swallow it. Goodness knows where the bread had come from or how old it was; it could easily be mouldy. When Scrumpi objected Edna gave her another piece which Venus showed her how to throw to the ducks. This game appealed to Edna who rummaged in her bag for more bread and pulled out a five pound note. Venus pushed it back into Edna's bag, noticing as she did so that it was almost full of paper money. It was a shock to discover that this poor old woman was nothing of the kind. She must have collected her pension week after week, by habit, and spent hardly any of it. There were hundreds of pounds, perhaps thousands, in her bag. She was so frail that anyone could have mugged her, and even if they had, Edna would probably have been more worried about the loss of the bread for the ducks than all her money.

"Edna," began Venus, "I live at Number 6 in the Close, quite near to you. All our back yards have been cleared to be made into beautiful gardens; yours as well. Did you know?"

"Yes," replied Edna, looking hard at Venus. "They took my pram."

Venus was at a loss. "Your *pram* Edna?"

"You can have it for your baby."

"Thank you," said Venus, weakly, feeling that thanks were expected.

"It's a proper pram; not a little thing like that." Edna pointed to the buggy. "That's no good for a baby."

"You might be right." Venus felt the conversation should be continued before it dried up altogether. "Edna your garden is going to be made into a lovely place for you to sit in and enjoy the flowers and plants. You'll have a seat like this one and there'll be a little pool of water in the middle, for the birds."

Edna stopped throwing bread for a minute and looked at Venus. She was taking an interest in what she had been told and Venus felt she was making a break through.

"What about ducks?" she asked.

Venus was flustered. "Ducks need a pond, Edna. Your pool won't be big enough for ducks, but the sparrows will come and the other birds and you can feed them instead."

"I like *ducks*" said Edna, stubbornly, going back to feeding them.

"You can still come to the park to see the ducks, can't you?"

Edna thought for a minute. "You'll bring the baby?"

"Of course I will."

Edna's face creased into a smile and she took Scrumpi's fat little hand in hers. Scrumpi looked at her with her big brown eyes opened wide and gurgled happily. Once the moment had passed Venus set off back home. She had made contact with the elusive Edna at last, but it had left her feeling more concerned than ever. When the project was finished she would keep an eye on Edna to see if anything could be done for her.

As she crossed the road Venus noticed the rusty handles of an old pram sticking up above the rest of the junk removed from Edna's garden and decided to have the skip removed at the earliest opportunity in case Edna mentioned it again and she felt obliged to accept it.

She pushed Scrumpi along by the fence which bordered Edna's backyard and looked over the top. William was busy laboriously planting out box hedging along the edge of one of the plots.

"How are you doing, William?"

"Oh hi, Venus; this is taking for ever. There are hundreds of these edging plants but it looks nice doesn't it? I didn't think it would look as good as this."

"You're doing a great job. It's an interesting pattern isn't it?"

William stood up and stretched his aching back. He was thick set, like his father, but had his mother's placid temperament which showed in his moonlike features.

"It's back breaking, but I'm enjoying it now it's taking shape. I didn't think I would at first, but I needed the money. When are the other plants coming? I've planted the triangles, but the other shapes will take longer."

"I'll ask Ed about it and let you know. Put a note through my door as to how many hours you've worked so far and he'll send you the money. We don't expect you to wait until it's all finished. That might take some time as you only have the weekends and after school is over for the day."

"Thanks. I haven't seen the old lady yet. Will she mind me being here?"

"I doubt she'll even notice you but she knows about it. I've just seen her in the park and spoken to her so she shouldn't cause you any trouble."

"I'd best get on; it'll take hours to get all this lot in."

Venus stood and watched him for a few moments as Scrumpi had fallen asleep in the pushchair. William was keeping strictly to Julian's white lines and she felt pleased he was taking so much trouble. He had finished planting the triangles; nasturtiums in one corner for the earth and blue catmint in the other to represent air; Lady's Mantle in the opposite corner for water and opposite that, red leaved basil for fire. She decided to ask William to take visitors round the healing garden when they were opened to the public to explain the planting pattern. She wanted Ed to show William in some of his shots. Linda would be so thrilled to see William on the television and one never knew but perhaps Alice would see her brother on the programme and it might inspire her to get in touch with home.

Benji was up when Venus arrived back home, trying to type out a recipe on the laptop with fingers that were too big for the keys and getting more and more frustrated.

"Where've you two been, may I ask? Thought I'd lost you. Have you bought up the parade today?"

The Hidden Gardens

"You'd never guess, Benji. We've been sitting chatting to Edna in the park and our Scrumpi's been feeding the ducks, haven't you sweetheart."

"Well, well! Did you get anywhere with her? Does she understand what's going to happen to her backyard?"

"I think so, but it's odd, Benji; she was in the post office drawing out *two* pensions when I saw her."

"Perhaps she was getting one for somebody else."

"Yes, but whom? Her bag is full of money. She gave Scrumpi a five pound note by mistake to give to the ducks, without noticing it wasn't a piece of bread."

"Lucky ducks!" Benji raised his eyebrows and pulled a face to make Scrumpi laugh.

"But she's walking about with all that money, Benji, hundreds of pounds, maybe thousands. She's not poor at all. I don't think she understands money."

"Obviously not; and who's trusting her with their pension, I wonder."

"I wondered that; and another thing; perhaps the house really does belong to her and we've got Edna all wrong. She might not be a squatter after all. She seemed quite indignant about her old pram being removed from the backyard; she even offered it to me for Scrumpi; that rusty old thing in the skip."

Benji roared with laughter. "Looked as if she needed it, did she?"

"Well, as a matter of fact she had something there; said the buggy was too small for a baby. Those old prams were built like armoured cars with every comfort added. There was no way of folding them up to put in a car boot; things have come a long way since those days but I don't expect Edna would know anything about that."

"So she can communicate then."

"Yes, but not for long; she can't concentrate; she forgets things and gets muddled."

"It's just old age; lots of people get like that as they're getting older."

"I know that, but this is different somehow. She lives in another world. She can't possibly look after herself in that broken down house. There's something odd about the whole business and I'm worried now in case she really does have a right to live there. We just presumed she was a squatter when we cleared out the backyard."

"She made no objection did she? Well then, I shouldn't worry. You're giving her a beautiful garden instead of a tip; she should be grateful."

"She mentioned the pram as if we had no right to have it removed. I can't help it Benji, I feel as if we've made a terrible mistake. Before I speak to Ed about it I'm going to speak to everyone in The Close to see if anyone can remember Edna from the past, although I rather doubt it. People move house more often these days."

"Stop worrying, my lovely, it was a wonderful idea and nobody is going to spoil it for you, least of all Edna."

There was a knock at the door and Linda stood there with a bag of clean washing.

"Sorry to bother you, Venus, but you didn't come back for your washing so I thought I'd just drop it in on my way home."

Venus was full of apologies. "Oh my goodness! I've never forgotten that before; thank you, Linda. Can you come in for a minute, there's something I want to ask you. I was coming round but now you're here—."

Linda came into the hallway but wouldn't come any further.

"I can't stop; you see it's Malcolm; he likes his dinner on the table as soon as he comes in and I've just bought some fish and chips."

"I only wanted to ask you about Edna. That's why I forgot to collect the washing. I saw her getting her pension from the post office and followed her into the park, so I could tell her about her backyard being made into a garden in case she got bothered when she saw William there."

"He was a bit bothered about that himself."

"Well, she understands what's being done, but I got the feeling that she's not a squatter and she has a right to live there."

The Hidden Gardens

"Never! I can't believe it; living in that slum. She's been coming in and out ever since we've lived next door but we never thought she lived there. She looks as if she hasn't got a penny to her name. Nobody else ever goes round there so she couldn't be paying rent for that hovel, could she?"

"No, of course not; but before we put the programme out we have to find out that we've done nothing illegal, and we haven't been able to trace the owner so we just went ahead with it."

"Oh, I do hope you do—go ahead with it I mean; it would be dreadful if you didn't complete all of the gardens just because of Edna," said Linda, thinking of William's job. "She wouldn't *own* it, would she? That's impossible; so she has no right to say what happens round the back. I shouldn't worry about it if I was you. Just forget about Edna and let William get on with things. He loves it. Says he'll go in for gardening when he leaves school; sorry, Venus, but I must go. Malcolm will be in any moment."

"Of course, and thanks a lot."

Venus was thoughtful as she bathed Scrumpi and put her in her cot. She'd go round and ask Linda if she'd baby sit a bit later on while she called on the other residents of Park Close. Before she spoke to Ed about her worries she must find out how long Edna had been living in Number 12, if such a thing was possible.

With Benji gone to work and Linda babysitting, Venus set off to pay a visit to each of her neighbours.

Damian ushered her into his small, tastefully furnished front room, apologising for Guy's absence.

"He works so hard you know on this project. The channels have to be tiled up the sides and along the water course and it's taking for ever. Fortunately he has the help of the work force but it's still hard for him, poor Guy."

"Are you pleased with the result?"

"Oh, yes indeed. We love it. Come and have a look next Saturday if you can, it's too dark outside at the moment. Guy will be here; working away no doubt."

"I really came to ask you if you had heard anything about Edna since you came to live here. She's a bit of a mystery, and as

Jan Pollard

we've decided to do a makeover of her backyard it's important that we find out a bit about her."

"No, I only know that people think she's a squatter. Nobody knows anything about her."

Venus promised she would look in next Saturday afternoon and pressed on to Number 4 only to find that the Fairweathers had been there only four months longer than her own family. They knew nothing, so she called on Millie.

Millie was pleased to tell Venus all she knew which was more than the others.

"I lived in this house as a child," explained Millie, "and I remember that a married couple lived there then. They kept to themselves and had nothing to do with their neighbours."

"Did you know their name? That might help."

"Can't really remember but I know it sounded foreign, which might be why they kept to themselves. My parents came here in the eighties, and later my grandfather came to live with them. I moved away and lived at Hendon with Lucy's father and then came back to live with my parents when she was born and I've lived here ever since."

"How long do you think Edna's been living at Number 12?"

"Well, she's been squatting there for as long as I've been here with Lucy. The house has got worse and worse; kids have broken the windows and thrown things into the backyard from the alley way. I'm glad you're making a garden there but the house needs doing up more than the garden."

"Do you know when the people with the foreign sounding name moved out? We've been trying to trace the owners without success."

"No idea. My mother never mentioned that they'd gone, but we just presumed they had left. Nobody seemed to live there except for Edna and she arrived about fifteen years ago, she's just a long term squatter; nobody to bother about."

Venus wished she could have tracked down the previous tenants of Number 10, who might have lived there during the time of Millie's parents, but she doubted that would be possible, and anyway it was too time consuming. They could have died or emigrated; there was no way of knowing; but they would have seen furniture being moved out and new owners moving in, living next door.

Venus returned home none the wiser, to find Linda sitting next to Scrumpi's cot and playing with her.

"I heard her on the baby alarm," explained Linda, looking guilty. "I guess she's teething."

Scrumpi looked very wide awake and not at all miserable. Venus wondered if Linda had woken her up on purpose to play with her, but she had no way of telling that. She knew Linda adored the baby

"I'll be off then, Venus. Ask me any time. I love looking after her."

"Do you mind seeing yourself out, Linda? I'll have to calm her down or we'll get no sleep tonight."

As she rocked the cot, Venus thought about Edna and what Millie had told her.

'Would a squatter own a pension book?' she wondered. The whole business was very puzzling.

CHAPTER 9

After hearing Venus discuss her concerns about the garden at Number 12, Ed decided to continue with the scheme as planned. Too much money had been invested already to change anything. Time was passing and plants needed to be put in place or the array of colour he intended to film during the summer months would not be forthcoming. Ed invited Beatrice Thorn to return to give advice to the residents about suitable plants for their type of garden, and to assist them with the purchase if necessary.

Beatrice got in touch with Ruth as soon as she heard she was returning and Ruth immediately invited her to stay. Mike objected strongly. He had hoped that now the summer term had started, with Ruth out of the way, he could continue to see Millie.

With Beatrice around his visits next door would no longer remain a secret from his wife, and at the moment he was unsure of how Millie felt about him. Once he knew where he stood with her he could sort out his relationship with Ruth and arrange a separation. But since the wretched Julian had spent time with her Mike was unsure of everything. Their tenuous friendship appeared to have cooled off and he was anxious to renew it in a far more meaningful way. He had been a fool not to have made his feelings for her more obvious from the start, but he had been afraid of her rejection.

"It will be so much easier for Beatrice if she's on the spot; surely you understand that, Mike; and we get along so well, Beatrice and me."

"I'm not moving out of my office for her or sleeping downstairs on the couch."

"I'm not asking you to. She can share the front room with me. Your single bed is still in there. She'll be no trouble to anyone."

"Oh, very well then, but I hope she's not staying long. I can't bear the woman."

"That's very obvious!" said Ruth, huffily.

Beatrice duly arrived with very little luggage, making Mike think it was only for a short stay. Ruth had made a great fuss about her arrival, cleaning and polishing until the house was spotless. The freezer had been filled with food of every description so Beatrice could eat whatever took her fancy. Nothing was too good for her it would seem. Mike had never known such a fuss. Ruth had gone way over the top with her preparations.

The weekend was an agony with Beatrice making all the conversation in her loud deep voice, and Ruth laughing at all her remarks in a silly girlish way. Beatrice disliked television; it was nothing but rubbish these days, according to her; so the television was never switched on. There was to be no respite from her. Mike went for a long walk and left them together. When he returned Beatrice was a bit quieter and Ruth had a smug look on her face. He got the feeling that they had been talking about him and went up to his office to be alone.

On Monday, after Ruth had left for school, Beatrice had plans to visit all the gardens and the residents when they were at home at whatever time of the day.

"I'm starting next door," she announced. "I've brought the young woman there a catalogue of rose bushes so she can choose the ones she would like for her flower beds."

"I'll take it round to her," said Mike, firmly, "and I'll take her to the nursery to choose them. That will save you some trouble at least. I'm sure you have a lot you'd rather be getting on with."

"Well, yes, there are a lot of gardens here and they need planting now. Tell her to choose no more than six bushes to a bed, and she'll need a rambler for the trellis."

Beatrice gave him a searching look as she left. He had seemed determined to go round next door. Perhaps there was something going on, although Ruth had never mentioned it. It would suit her if there was, for Beatrice wanted Ruth all to herself.

Mike went round to Millie's back door and was glad to see there were no customers in her salon. Too early for that he supposed. Millie asked him in, surprised to see him, and put the kettle on for coffee.

"Long time, no see," said Millie.

"I've missed you, Millie. Thought you didn't want to see me anymore, so I didn't want to embarrass you by coming round; but I've brought you this, from dear Beatrice."

"You never embarrass me, Mike; I love seeing you."

"Just as a friend though; that's it, isn't it, Millie?"

"Only while Lucy's in your wife's class. I've explained that to you before."

"How long will that be?"

"About five weeks now."

"And then—?"

"It might be different then."

"How, like this?"

Mike got up from his seat and pulled her into his arms. She seemed to melt in his embrace and put her arms round his neck and kissed him on the lips. Mike, who had longed for this moment began to kiss her passionately and started to undo the buttons on her blouse, but before he could touch her breasts she pushed him away.

"I can't now; you know I can't now. Please Mike, try to understand. I want you to make love to me but it's got to be right, at the right time; not like this."

"Is it because of Julian, Millie? Is that why you can't love me?"

Millie looked startled; how could he have known what had gone on between her and Julian.

"He's just a Romeo, lurking around to pick up a nice girl like you. He's a sexual pest who preys on vulnerable women. I saw how he looked at you at the resident's meeting. It was obvious what he wanted."

"He came here once to discuss the garden; Lucy's garden."

Mike felt deflated. "I'm sorry, Millie. Please forgive me; I'd never say anything to upset you; I presumed too much. You're so perfect, so lovely and everything I've ever dreamed of in a woman and I couldn't bear the thought of that man laying his hands—."

"Stop it! I don't want to hear it; never talk about it again; do you hear?"

"Of course I won't, ever, and that's a promise."

Mike wanted to hold her in his arms again and calm her down, but Millie kept away.

The memory of Julian and the afternoon they had spent together in an orgy of love making had disturbed her. She wanted to keep that to herself. She wished now that it had never happened but she had felt unable to control her feelings and had found herself swept away on a tide of emotions which she had suppressed for far too long. At the time she had found it a wonderful release but now Mike was here she regretted it.

Mike felt there must have been something going on as Millie had become so agitated, but it appeared to be over now. He had had many affairs of his own in the past. Some had lasted for a while and some had been the briefest of encounters but none had been of a serious nature as he had wanted no permanent involvement. He had enjoyed his bachelor status and the fact that with his good looks he could have anyone he wanted. He had fallen in love with Millie. It was different this time and he wanted to think of her as above that kind of carnal love. Millie was his perfect woman. She existed to be worshipped and loved as only he could love her.

Mike got up to leave and placed the catalogue in Millie's hand.

Jan Pollard

"Beatrice wants you to choose six roses for each of your rose beds and a rambler for the trellis. They have to be planted very soon now, so if you would like me to, I'll take you to the nursery in my car to collect them and plant them for you. I promised I'd help you to do that, if you remember."

"I remember."

"You'll let me take you, won't you; I've been looking forward to it; spending a day with you."

"All right; I'll come with you to-morrow. I haven't got any customers then. They usually come at the end of the week." Millie smiled at him. "Cheer up; you're forgiven."

Mike kissed her cheek gently as he left. "We're still friends, then?"

"Yes, still friends."

Mike returned home to find Beatrice shifting a huge stone into place amongst the gravel.

"Want any help, Beatrice?"

"No thanks," was her frosty reply.

Beatrice was a power house of energy. There seemed to be no limits to her ability to lift huge slabs and stones and put them in place. The workforce stood in awe of her; it was like having a tornado in their midst. Gerry found he was no longer able to take an extended break in Number 8 with Guy. The other two men in his team had become used to his absence for far longer than was permitted, and just carried on with the jobs on their own. As a result the work proceeded slowly and would never have been finished in the time allotted to them.

Beatrice soon put a stop to that! She wanted to know why Venus and Benji's backyard had not been paved by now. The terracotta tiles were still waiting to be laid where the scrubby lawn had once been, and where a large decking area for the barbecue was to be built. The play area for Scrumpi was finished but that was all. The concrete had been coloured in pale orange and featured shell shapes and large round ammonites, making a fun area for her to run over and ride her small tricycle around when she was a little older. There was a flat area ready for a swing and a climbing frame, which had protective latex mixed into it, for safety.

"All very charming," remarked Beatrice when she first saw it, "a typical Julian design; artistic, but not altogether practical. The rest of the garden should have been finished by now. It has to be planted and plants need time to get established. I have to get borders filled with top soil and treated with fertilisers first. What on earth have you been doing? You've had weeks and nothing is properly finished."

The men looked at each other with grins on their faces. They had a pretty good idea as to what Gerry had been doing and it certainly wasn't work. They had done their best but three men were better than two when jobs needed to be done.

"Just look at all these tiles! Leave what you're doing today and get this lot down. I can't do anything with these borders as it is at present."

Benji came out to see what all the fuss was about.

"Hey! Hey! Beatrice; give them a break. They're doing their best."

"I doubt that. I doubt that very much. Your garden should be ready for planting by now, and just look at it. It's a wasteland."

Benji went back indoors. For his wife's sake he felt he should keep out of it. He knew Venus thought the work force was inefficient herself but they had a contract with the company and it was up to them to finish the work.

"The only work that seems to be finished are the water channels next door, and you've made a good job of them. The blue mosaic tiles take a long time to put down. I presume the residents gave a hand with that. I will need your help to site the fountain in front of the gazebo when Mr De Courcy and Mr Wentworth have chosen it. Right! Time to get back to work; I've stopped you for quite long enough."

"We're still working on the pergola at Number 2," objected Gerry. "Aren't we supposed to finish that first?"

"No, leave it and do this paving, the pergola can wait. I see you've finished the raised rose beds there. You used new railway

Jan Pollard

sleepers rather than second hand ones I noticed. More expensive but better in the long run. The old ones can let the water seep through eventually."

"Done something right, have we," said Gerry, sarcastically.

Beatrice strode off to see what Malcolm had been up to, presuming that he would be at work and she could have a good look round without any interference.

"Bloody woman!" said one of the men, when Beatrice had gone. "She's worse than my mother-in-law, and you should hear her, sometimes."

"*Woman,* she's more like the bloody sergeant major I had in the army, and we all hated him."

"No more swinging the lead, Gerry. We'll get on better with you around."

Gerry was indignant. "Who's been swinging the lead? You couldn't call having a cup of coffee with a friend, swinging the lead, could you?"

The men laughed. They knew all about Gerry and his men friends.

Guy, who had heard Beatrice, walked along the embankment to find Gerry.

"Anything wrong, chaps?"

The work force moved away and started mixing the base for the tiles, leaving Gerry to talk to him.

"That bloody woman; we'll have to keep going or we won't get finished on time. If she's keeping her beady eye on us I won't be able to come round any more, Guy."

"No more fun and games, then."

"No more anything, mate. Not while we're here. See ya tonight, and you can come round to mine later."

Guy, who had to be satisfied with that, went back into his garden only to be confronted with the large bulk of Beatrice before he reached the door.

"Ah, Mr De Courcy, you appeared to be out when I called. I'm glad to see you. Do you think you could spare the time to come with me to collect your planters and to choose the bushes to put in them, to-morrow? You can come in my car. I don't think you have one of your own." Beatrice gave him what she considered to be a winning smile.

Guy was fascinated by her huge mouth. He felt like a victim whom she was about to devour for her next meal. He had no wish to go with Beatrice in her car but perhaps he should if only to get the business over with, as Damian was always at the shop during the day and would never be free to go on these jaunts to the plant nursery.

Guy agreed with a sinking heart. They had looked at different kinds of planters in the catalogue Venus had left with them, and he knew which ones Damian wanted. As he intended leaving Damian before much longer Guy wanted Damian to have everything he had chosen. He was the one who would live with the Persian garden and Guy hoped it would still give him pleasure. He had the odd pang of remorse about leaving Damian but he had made up his mind. Gerry was a gift from the gods and Guy wanted to live in Morocco with him more than anything.

"We can look at the fountains while we're there," continued Beatrice. "Kill two birds with one stone, so to speak. You'll need a fountain in front of your gazebo; a Moorish garden should be full of water features; water has a calming influence."

Guy winced. He found the expression about the birds distasteful. He and Damian loved birds and listened to their songs on a tape as they sat in the gazebo on warm summer evenings. He hoped the water would have a calming influence on Damian when he was alone. Damian got so upset when things went wrong.

"What time do you suggest we leave to-morrow?"

"As early as possible; the nursery I have in mind is near Kew Gardens, so it's quite a drive. How about eight thirty?"

"That's fine."

"I'll see you then."

Guy decided not to tell Gerry he was spending the next day with Beatrice Thorn. He could imagine the ribbing there would be at his expense. Anyway Gerry wouldn't be visiting him anymore. Beatrice had put a stop to that, the interfering old spoilsport.

Jan Pollard

Beatrice left through the back of the garden and went to look at Malcolm's vegetables. He was nowhere to be seen so she presumed he was at work and there would be no objections to her looking around. She noticed that Malcolm had already edged his plots with short wooden stakes placed close together. They were expensive but she seemed to remember Julian telling him he could have what he wanted to take the heat out of an unpleasant situation, and Julian had suggested them originally, although she had quibbled about the price at the time. Julian never took price into consideration. He had designed gardens for the rich and famous in the past and price meant nothing to him; just the end result.

He had done the edging well, and planted his carrots and broad beans in straight lines and his early potatoes had been earthed up and looked very healthy. The grass paths had been laid between his plots and looked well cared for; there would be no grass seeding amongst his vegetables, despite all his complaints; he was too good a gardener for that.

In the greenhouse there were cucumbers coming up in pots and tomatoes, already staked, in the grow bags. The potting shed was tidy and well arranged with his tools carefully set out in racks and on shelves, and the pots neatly stacked one inside the other. Beatrice was impressed. She had some ideas to discuss with him but would leave that for a while. She had no wish to antagonise him while things were going so well.

She shut the door and turned her attention to the patio which his wife had wanted, only to see that nothing had been done. She would have to speak to that indolent work force yet again. It was too bad!

Beatrice went through the back and went to look at William's efforts in Edna's garden. There were two boxes of plants on the path waiting to be planted that needed watering. She had heard that William had very little time for the job and decided to get on with putting them in, but first she would need a small gardening fork and a trowel and a watering can. She decided to borrow Malcolm's which she had seen in his shed, as he was nowhere to be seen, and she had noticed a water butt beside

Edna's back door. That would do splendidly; rain water was better for plants than tap water any day.

William had drawn a plan on the fence in chalk, and had marked the plots with numbers so he knew where to put the plants as they arrived. What a sensible boy; now she knew exactly where to put these plants as each box was numbered. Beatrice set to work. It was a beautiful warm spring day and a pleasure to be working in the garden. In the first plot she planted what appeared to be marjoram, peppermint and basil, and in the second plot, which was a small rectangular shape, she planted coriander. When she had finished she filled the watering can from Edna's butt and watered the plants liberally. Then, on looking at the box hedging plants which bordered all the plots she decided to give them some water too. When she had finished to her satisfaction the water level had gone down considerably in the water butt.

Pleased with her mornings work Beatrice returned the items to Malcolm's potting shed and returned for her lunch. Mike was eating a ham sandwich in the kitchen.

"Ah," said Beatrice. "I'll have a couple of those; are they ham? I'm starving! I've been gardening most of the morning."

"Nice morning for it," remarked Mike, getting out the loaf of bread, butter and ham and putting them on the table. "Help yourself; there are plenty of other things in the fridge if you would like them. Ruth stocked up knowing you would be here."

He picked up his plate and mug to take upstairs. If Beatrice thought he was going to wait on her she had another think coming.

When Ruth arrived home from school that afternoon there were crumbs all over the table and dirty plates and knives in the sink.

"Mike!" she shouted, from the bottom of the stairs. "Why haven't you cleared up after yourself? I haven't got time to see to all your mess when I get home; I've got to begin preparing the dinner as soon as I get in."

Beatrice came in from the garden. "Ah Ruth my dear, sorry about the mess; I'm afraid that was me. I was too busy this afternoon in your garden to clear up once I'd finished lunch. I hope you don't mind."

"Oh, that's fine, Beatrice, really anything is fine by me." Ruth's voice sounded as if butter wouldn't melt in her mouth. It made Mike cringe to hear her speak to this domineering woman in such a way. The person he had married had become totally obsessed with another woman and he realised he had never really known her at all. It had been Ruth, who had made all the running after they had met, and Ruth who had wanted to get married, and Ruth who had hated any form of sexual approach once the honeymoon was over. He had never seen her reaction to another woman before and he wondered if perhaps she had suffered a broken relationship with a woman partner in the past, at the time of their meeting, or maybe she was bi-sexual, whatever it was he had been taken in completely by her. He had been unattached after a broken relationship and had found her attractive at first, always so smart and well dressed, and they had seemed to share the same interests, but perhaps she had been pretending all along. He had felt cheated once she made it clear that sex with him left her cold but now he realised he had never understood her or her physical needs and despite everything that had happened in the past he began to feel a twinge of pity for her. They were totally incompatible. Ruth wanted the love of another woman and that woman appeared to be Beatrice Thorn. A life with Millie became even more important to him now, and five more weeks seemed an eternity to wait.

Malcolm saw the watering can left outside his potting shed and knew someone had been around. He always put it beside the door and it had been left round the side. Inside the shed his small fork and trowel were in a completely different place from where he kept them. Nothing appeared to be missing but somebody had definitely been in there and he decided to keep the door padlocked in future.

"You haven't been in my shed, have you, Linda?"

"I wouldn't dare without your permission, now would I, you know me better than that."

"Well someone's used my things today and I want to know who."

"Funny that, when William got home from school he went round next door to see if his plants had been delivered and found that someone had already planted them. He was really upset. He'll lose money if someone else is doing his work for him."

"They must have used my things; the bloody cheek! I reckon it was that Nigerian woman, what's her name; I'm complaining to her when I've had me tea."

"She's Jamaican, Malcolm. I've told you that before, and her name's Venus. She's a very nice person and I'm sure it wasn't her."

"Well, I'm getting to the bottom of it, if it's the last thing I do."

Malcolm stormed round to Number 6 later, only to find that Venus knew nothing at all about it.

"Maybe it was Beatrice Thorn," she suggested. "She's helping out at the moment."

"Ah!" That made sense, and Malcolm decided to deal with her the next time they met.

Edna went to her water butt that evening to fill her kettle and discovered the water level had gone down considerably and she needed to stand on a chair to reach it. Perhaps that boy from next door was using it for his plants. When this had happened before, during a long dry spell of weather, she had filled her kettle from the drinking fountain in the park but that was far from easy and she hoped that would never be necessary again. Edna had no memory of a time when water had come out of her taps and anyway they were much too rusty now for her to turn them on.

"I hope you'll be free to-morrow afternoon, Guy. I've asked someone to come and look at Mummy's French writing desk and the chiffonier. I've decided to sell them and just heard there's a big sale soon of French antique furniture. They gave me a cancelled appointment for to-morrow afternoon and I don't want to miss the opportunity of getting a good price."

"Are you short of money, or perhaps I shouldn't ask."

"No nothing like that. I've wanted to get rid of them for a long time. They take up too much room in this tiny house and the chiffonier is such a heavy piece of furniture. I had hoped that one day we might move to a bigger house in a better area but now we have the Persian garden I expect we'll stay, don't you?"

Guy was unable to answer that; it made him feel terrible.

"Sorry, Damian; I don't know for sure that I'll be here but I can try. I have a date that I can't really break."

"Not with a woman, surely?"

"Yes indeed. The irresistible Beatrice has asked me to accompany her to the plant nursery at Kew. We start at eight thirty to-morrow morning and I can't wait!"

Damian roared with laughter. Guy looked the picture of misery.

"You had me worried for a moment. How are you getting there?"

"In her car it would seem. You must have seen it standing outside the Fairweather's house. That dirty old station wagon. It looks as if she carts compost around with her; I'm dreading it, I tell you"

"Poor you; what are you going for?"

"I have to choose the planters and the bushes to go in them, and choose a fountain to stand outside the gazebo, although they will send that I would think. It shouldn't take all day and I'll tell her about your visitor coming so she knows I have to get back."

"That'll be a good excuse for you to get away. I'll ask him to wait for a little if you're not back."

"Oh, I shall be back if I have anything to do with it."

Damian came and put his arm round Guy's shoulders. He could always rely on Guy. He loved and trusted him implicitly. Guy would never let him down.

CHAPTER 10

The inside of Beatrice's car had a strange smell. The leather seats were torn in places and Guy noticed there were half eaten apple cores rotting inside the open glove compartment. Being very fastidious himself it was all he could do not to throw up as they hurtled along the road to Kew, with Guy being jerked violently backwards and forwards as Beatrice changed gear. She kept up a running commentary, criticising the lack of competence of the other drivers as they went along, and shouting at them occasionally through her open window if she felt they deserved it. Guy hoped nobody thought he was anything to do with her and feared they might become involved in a case of road rage when an irate driver left his car and approached in a threatening manner. Seeing the driver was a woman he thought better of it and once the traffic moved on Beatrice moved on with it. Guy breathed a sigh of relief. It had been a terrible experience and he began to dread the journey home before they had even arrived, having impressed upon Beatrice the necessity of getting back early in the afternoon. Hopefully there would be less traffic about with it not being the rush hour.

Once at the nursery at Kew the square wooden planters were soon discovered and then came the trudge round to find suitable bushes to put in them. Damian had wanted small ornamental

Jan Pollard

orange trees but without the means for protecting them from the frosty weather they were impractical. Beatrice suggested clipped box trees and Guy agreed with that idea although he would not be around to do any of the clipping to keep them in shape.

Guy struggled round with one trolley while Beatrice pushed the heavier one containing most of the planters. They needed twelve to stand three on each side of the two water channels which would be connected to the main channel, and they filled the two trolleys. Beatrice decided it would be best to take them back to the car first before they went to look for a fountain. It was a long walk back to the car and as they loaded up another car drew up beside them in the car park. Guy recognised the occupants as Millie Carrington and Mike Fairweather. It seemed odd that they should be visiting the nursery together but maybe he was giving her a lift to collect her plants as well.

Mike cursed when he realised which car was parked next to him. It was bad enough living in the same house as Beatrice but worse still meeting her like this. Now Ruth would be told he had brought Millie out with him without telling her, and she had a cruel tongue when she liked. Millie worried about Ruth taking it out on Lucy and was all for returning home immediately, but Mike refused saying it made no difference now. Beatrice knew he was bringing her to collect her roses at some time. It just happened to be the wrong time which was unfortunate. Perhaps Beatrice and Guy would soon be finished and they could spend the rest of the time together without interruption.

The fountain was fairly easy to find as since the popularity of the Islamic garden at a previous Chelsea Flower Show there had been considerable interest shown in such a shape. Beatrice ordered a smaller version, with a wide bowl and a small fount of water bubbling over in the centre and spilling over the edges into the bowl below. Guy almost wished he would still be around to enjoy it from the gazebo but he imagined there would be beautiful Moorish gardens to admire in Morocco, apart from other pleasures.

Beatrice chose a selection of bush roses for flower beds close to the water, and four small cherry trees to plant on the lawns that bordered the channels. Guy could see he was going to be kept busy planting everything before he left. He would *need* a holiday once it was all finished!

By the time they arrived back at the car Beatrice had picked up four sacks of assorted stones to edge the water channels, and for the water from the fountain to trickle over.

Guy began to wonder if the station wagon would take the weight as he pushed everything inside, struggling with a sack of stones which fell back on his feet. Beatrice rescued him and picked them up as if they weighed nothing.

"You're out of condition, Mr De Courcy," she remarked, as she pushed the door shut. "Come along, now. Time we were off or we won't be back in time for your appointment."

Guy found he was sharing his seat with the roots of four cherry trees, the tops of which were threaded through the sun roof. Although there was very little space for him at least he was so jammed in the violent gear changes made far less impact on his person, and the open top of the car made the smell inside less obvious. They returned to the Close in good time, and as far as Guy was concerned, with a sense of relief.

It had been wonderful to have Millie sitting beside him, in a world all of their own, as Mike and Millie travelled together towards Kew. They said very little; it seemed unnecessary to make conversation as just being together in happy companionship was enough for the present.

When they had arrived and found they had parked the car next to Beatrice's station wagon it had been a terrible shock, but Mike had managed to calm Millie's fears by explaining that he had already arranged to bring her with Beatrice's knowledge. He omitted to tell her that he had not told Ruth, but then he told Ruth very little these days. No doubt Beatrice would tell her and he would face that when it happened.

Once Beatrice and Guy had moved away to finish whatever they were shopping for, Mike took Millie in the opposite direction to look for her rose bushes. There were hundreds of roses to choose from and Millie was in her element. She wanted to plant her roses in beds of one colour and chose six of different shades of each colour to put in each bed. Mike loaded them on a long trolley as she gave them to him. They had such wonderful names and the labels promised beautiful blooms for the summer months.

Right at the end, Millie chose a white rambler rose to cover the trellis and the archway into Lucy's garden.

"Look at this, Mike, its called Kiftsgate; it's a rampant climbing rose with creamy white flowers and will soon make Lucy's garden into a very private place."

Her pleasure was infectious, and Mike began to look forward to the time when he could see the transformation of Millie's garden into a rose bower.

"Aren't you going to grow anything else apart from roses? They don't flower all the year round you know."

"Well, there's the pergola to think about. I'll have to find some really large pots for climbing plants, so they can grow up the posts. Let's see what we can find."

In due course some enormous blue pots were found. Millie decided to buy four, and found a purple clematis and an early pink clematis to put in them. A white montana and a honeysuckle concluded her purchases. The pots were too large for Mike's small Fiat and it was arranged for them to be delivered when the fountain was to be sent to the Close. Beatrice had arranged for all the plants to come from the same nurseries and to be charged to the television company. It was a most enjoyable way to do the shopping.

Mike lifted the roses into the boot of his car and looked at some of the labels. Lovely Lady and Maiden's Blush were two of the ones Millie had chosen. Mike thought they were magical names and described her perfectly.

Beatrice and Guy had long since gone but Mike had no wish to return to the Close yet. He wanted to linger longer with Millie.

"How about I take you to see Kew Gardens now we're so close; no comparison to ours of course, but they are really beautiful."

"Thanks, I'd really like that; I've never been before."

"Then it's time you went. The rhododendrons are magnificent, the most wonderful colours you can imagine, but it's too early for them; they need a few more weeks. I'll take you to see them and the azaleas when they're out, but there are plenty of other things to see; the huge glass houses for one."

Millie loved the gardens, the space and the displays of late spring flowers. They wandered down the paths hand in hand, exploring the different paths, until they came to a wide, open vista. An enormous pagoda stood at the end surrounded by the pink blossom of Japanese cherry trees, looking just as if the top was emerging from clouds.

"Isn't that beautiful, Mike. Have you ever seen such a sight! Wouldn't you like that in your garden?"

"What, a great thing like that! No I would not. It's bad enough having a teahouse. I'm not doing anything about that, it's entirely in the hands of my wife and her buddy Beatrice. I hope they know what they're doing because it's beyond me and they've made it clear that they don't want my help. In fact I'm just in the way. Beatrice has taken over."

Millie put her arms round his waist and rested her head on his shoulder. Mike bent to kiss the top of her silky blonde head.

"I wish we could stay like this for ever, Millie. I love you; you know that."

"I want to take you home with me, Mike. It's awful that you have to go back there but I can't until—."

"I know; I understand. Once Beatrice is out of the way I'll speak to Ruth about a divorce. I can't see her making any objections. She's totally wrapped up in that woman and has no time for anything else."

"Do you think it's that kind of a relationship?"

"I've begun to wonder. Ruth has changed so much. She seems to be happy now so perhaps that was what she always wanted; another woman. They share her bedroom and Ruth is totally dominated by her. I thought she was coming to stay for a few weeks but somehow I think she's there for keeps. I can't stay if she does. The house belongs to both of us so I'll have to sort that out with a solicitor."

"Well, I'm not far away."

Mike kissed her. She was so sweet and lovely and the best thing that had happened to him in his whole life. The trouble was that she might have been a thousand miles away for all he could do about it. He had to respect her feelings for Lucy's happiness, and he would wait for as long as it took.

Millie took hold of his hand.

"Time to go home, Mike. I wish we could have stayed here for much longer but I have to fetch Lucy; you know how it is."

Mike knew only too well. Lucy had been a stumbling block in their relationship up to now, and he would need to win Lucy over before the way was clear to living with her mother, and that might be difficult.

"Beatrice tells me she saw you this morning with Millie Carrington, Mike. Have you been having an affair with her behind my back?" asked Ruth, on his return home.

Mike was ready for her. He had been expecting something like this.

"And I saw Beatrice with Guy De Courcy, Ruth. Perhaps they've been having an affair that you knew nothing about."

"Don't be ridiculous! Sometimes you make me sick, Mike."

"Beatrice knew I was taking Millie to choose her roses; I told her the other day. You'd already gone when we left and I'd forgotten to mention it to you. I hardly ever see you these days to tell you anything, as you well know."

Ruth shrugged off the remark.

"Well, now you *are* here, I have some news to tell you which might be of interest."

She had the same smug look on her face that he remembered seeing when he had returned from his walk, after Beatrice had arrived to stay.

"Well, what is it?"

"I gave in my notice at the beginning of the term. I won't be going back in September."

"I thought you were looking for a better job. You won't get one like that."

"I've got a better job and one that suits me far more than teaching."

"What's that, then?"

"I'm going to be Beatrice's secretary."

Mike thought it might have had something to do with Beatrice. The woman seemed to have brain washed his wife.

"Does she need a secretary?"

"Of course, or she wouldn't have asked me. She has lecture tours booked for most of next year all over the world, and I shall be going with her. I shall have my expenses paid by the people who book her services. She's very well known in the world of horticulture *and* she's an authority on Japanese gardens."

"I'd never have guessed," sighed Mike.

Ruth warmed to her subject.

"We have an extra day's holiday tomorrow because of the Bank Holiday so we're going to the last day of the Chelsea Flower Show. They have a Japanese garden there which has won a gold medal and Beatrice wants to see it. She's determined to win the prize for our garden when it's finished."

"I don't somehow think it's *our* garden Ruth. You've got that wrong."

"That's right, pick me up on some little thing rather than be pleased for me. That's just like you, Mike."

"I am pleased for you Ruth, and pleased for the poor kids you taught. It'll be a relief for them to have another teacher rather than one who gives them nightmares."

"How dare you! I was a *good* teacher! I had an excellent report from the Ofsted inspectors. There was no bad behaviour in my classroom. I could keep control which is more than a lot of them can these days."

"I'm sure you could, but they're little kids, Ruth. You would have been better teaching in a comprehensive. They need to be controlled at that age."

"You don't understand, Mike. All kids are big trouble these days, ask anyone. They rule the world, or think they do. Parents are putty in their hands; they hold them to ransom to get what they want; designer clothes, computers, mobile phones, you name it, they'll have it whatever the cost."

"I don't expect they're all like that."

"How would you know? You've never had any."

It was a cruel cut. Ruth knew he had wanted children when they had married. She had been the one to deny him sexual satisfaction and had made it clear afterwards that she disliked children and never intended to have any. He would be glad to see the back of her and Beatrice Thorn. They deserved one another.

"I want to talk to you, Ruth, about this so called marriage of ours. I want it ended and I'm sure you do too. There's no point in us going on like this."

"I couldn't agree more, but this isn't the time to discuss it. I need to speak to Beatrice first."

"What has she got to do with it?"

"She's got everything to do with it, Mike. You wouldn't understand so there's no point in discussing it with you."

"Discussing what?"

"Love, Mike, love. You don't know the meaning of the word."

Mike turned away from her. What ever had he seen in this woman?

"Just let me know when you're ready to talk about this, Ruth, and make it sooner than later. Divorce takes time to arrange and living here with you two is impossible, but my work is here and I intend to stay, so you'd better discuss that with her too."

"Beatrice will be finished here soon until the gardens open to the public. We're going to Japan for a holiday when the term ends, so she won't be around much more. She has a flat in Ealing and I shall be spending my weekends there with her. You can make whatever arrangements you like for the weekends, and see your little girlfriend from next door for all I care. You're welcome to her; I've told you what kind of woman she is, you're a fool, Mike."

Mike refused to be goaded any further. He felt certain that Ruth would regret her decision to live with Beatrice Thorn. She was a greedy woman and would probably finish with her once

The Hidden Gardens

she had got all she could out of her, but that was their business. Another life beckoned for him and he longed for that to begin. It had been a relief to get this discussion out of the way and to know exactly where he stood with Ruth. Once they had gone to Chelsea he would plant Millie's roses for her and spend the day next door.

It took Mike most of the morning, apart from a break for coffee, to sort out which roses were to go in which bed and to plant them. When he began on the white rambler for the trellis, he was surprised to find Lucy watching him. He realised that she must have been standing there for some time before he was aware of her presence. Mike stopped work to talk to her. He was anxious to make a good impression for without Lucy's approval he would never get any further with her mother. He had heard that children could wreck a marriage and Millie had been very important to Lucy all her young life. Sharing her mother with Mike might not go down too well.

"It's nice to meet you, Lucy. What do you think of your rose hedge? It's going to grow very quickly so you'll soon have your garden all to yourself."

"What colour are they?"

"Here you are; look at the picture on the label. This is what it will look like in no time at all."

"They're white! I didn't want a white hedge. I wanted a pink one."

"Oh, dear, I'm sorry about that. I don't think we can change it now; I've planted half of them. You should have told your mother then we'd have found a pink one for you."

"Did you go with my Mum then, to get the roses?"

"Yes, I took her in my car. It would have been very difficult for her to go unless someone took her, and it would have been hard for her to plant all these, so I said I'd put them in for her. I hope she'll like them. They'll look beautiful when they all come out; just like your Mum."

There was a bit of a pause while Lucy summed him up, and Mike went on digging.

"You're not like Mrs Fairweather. I don't like her."

"No, I know you don't, but you won't have Mrs Fairweather much longer. She's leaving your school for good. She's not going to be a teacher any longer."

"All the kids will be glad about that when I tell them."

"I should keep it a secret, Lucy; our secret. She might get mad if she knows I've told you, and that could be difficult for both of us."

"Does she get mad with you too, Mr Fairweather?"

"Just occasionally; and call me, Mike; it's much better than Mr Fairweather."

"O.K."

Lucy gave him a smile as she left and Mike felt as if he had made a propitious start, even if the roses were the wrong colour.

Millie's last customer for the day had gone and she came out into the garden to see how he was getting on.

"Stay and eat with us, Mike. You seem to have broken the ice with Lucy. She tells me your wife is leaving the school for good. That's put a smile on her face."

"Perhaps I shouldn't have told her. If she tells the others Ruth might not like it."

"She won't, she says it's your secret. It's made her feel very important."

"Ruth's leaving teaching altogether. She only told me yesterday. Apparently she's going to be Beatrice Thorn's secretary and travel the world with her. You were right about their relationship; it's made it easier to discuss a divorce. It's what she wants too so it should go through without any problem. Then I'll be free, Millie, free!"

Mike picked her up and swung her round until she was breathless with laughter. He had just begun to kiss her when Lucy came to the door to call her mother to the telephone.

"Who is it, sweetheart? Did they say?"

"It's a man; he said he's my Daddy. But he can't be my Daddy can he? My Daddy's dead; you told me he'd died a long time ago."

Mike felt fear clutch at his heart. Millie looked shocked as she pulled away from him and ran indoors to answer the 'phone.

He had almost finished the job when she returned, looking worried, and he took her in his arms to comfort her.

"Did you know the man? Was he Lucy's father?"

Millie nodded. "I didn't tell her the truth about him, that's the worst part. She kept asking me about her father as she was growing up and I didn't want to hurt her by telling her he had never wanted her and had left me before she was born. It seemed easier to say he had died; well he might well have done as far as we were concerned. He was dead to me. I had no feelings for him; in fact I hated him and never wanted to see him again. He put me off men for good, or so I thought."

Mike stroked her hair and held her close to him. She was shaking with sobs.

"You don't feel like that now, do you Millie?" he asked, gently.

She flung her arms round him and kissed him.

"I don't know what I'd have done without you, Mike. You've shown me what it is to be loved and you've understood about Lucy; I can never thank you enough for that. Any other man would have given up on me by now."

"I'll never do that, Millie. I want to spend the rest of my life with you if you feel the same way about me."

"Of course I do, and I want you so much, but you know how it is."

Mike sighed. He knew only too well and wanting her too was driving him crazy.

"Where's Lucy, by the way? Have you told her the truth?"

"Only a part of it; I've told her it *was* her father and that he wants to come and see us. He has a right to see her if he wants to even if he had nothing to do with bringing her up. He's been making enquiries and knows he is legally entitled to see her."

"How does Lucy feel about that?"

"Oh, she's thrilled to find she has a father, but furious with me. She's gone up to her room to write a letter to him, full of childish love and affection no doubt without understanding anything about it. I'm in the dog house at present. When she's older I'll have to explain to her how he walked out on us before she was born and even wanted me to have an abortion. She might love him when she gets to know him and if they have a bond then I won't tell her the truth until she's ready for it."

Mike was angry seeing her placed in such an impossible position after all she had done for her child. How dare this man arrive out of the blue and take possession of his daughter's affection when he had cared so little for her mother, and nothing at all for the baby she was expecting. Life was so unfair sometimes.

"I'd better go back I suppose. I've done as much as I can here for the moment."

"Oh, don't go, Mike. There's no need to go; really. I want you to stay to lunch. It's only a salad I'm afraid, nothing special, but I invited you and I haven't any other customers today. I was going to take Lucy for a picnic down the tow path at the Grand Union Canal. She always liked that, and we loved watching the narrow boats. If she still wants to come then please come with us. I'd like you to."

"Well, if you're sure. I'd love to come. I haven't been along the canal for years. How do you get there from here without a car?"

"It's quite easy really. We take a bus and then walk to get to the canal. Money has always been short so our treats have had to be simple ones but we've enjoyed them just the same."

"I'll give you a treat this time. We'll go in my car, and then we can see more of the canal before we have our picnic. Save you going on the bus."

Millie smiled at him. He was always so thoughtful; he was wasted on that miserable wife of his. Soon she would be able to show him how much she really loved him. She wanted Lucy to love him too so they could be a real family, but first she would have to sort out Lucy's father. If he only wanted to see her occasionally that shouldn't be too much of a problem. She wouldn't know until she had met him and they had sorted something out between them.

After lunch Mike helped her to make the sandwiches and pack the basket, and then went to fetch the car. Ruth and Beatrice had driven to Chelsea in her old station wagon so they had room to bring back all the things they had their eye on when the plants were sold off.

It would leave them more cash to use from the television company, as many of the things Beatrice considered necessary for the garden were a fantastic price, especially the teahouse which the ground force were putting together to cut down on expense.

The huge blocks of sandstone to create the effect of mountains in the distance had been extremely expensive, and taken the ground force many weary hours of Beatrice's instructions to get them exactly into the right place. Mike was glad it had nothing to do with him when he caught sight of their miserable faces.

The ride in the car had pleased Lucy and she was in a better mood by the time they began their walk along the tow path. Lucy ran ahead and Mike took Millie's hand in his as they dawdled along. It was a lovely warm day in May and the people who passed them in the narrow boats looked happy as they chugged past. Mike wished there was nothing to stop him and Millie from feeling so at ease on such a perfect day.

"Well, what did Lucy's father suggest if you don't mind me asking?"

Millie sighed. She wished she could forget the whole thing. She felt so content with Mike and happier than she had been for years.

"He wants to come and stay with us next week so he can get to know her before she goes back to school."

"How do you feel about that, Millie? I don't like the sound of it. Why can't he stay elsewhere? Surely you don't have to put him up?"

"Of course not, but he asked very nicely. I'm doing it for Lucy, and it won't happen again. You don't have to worry, Mike. He's not sharing my bed under any circumstances. I have no feelings for *him* at all, only for you, and you'll be the one sharing my bed before much longer; you know that. He can sleep in a single bed in the student's room. They won't be there next week because of their half term holiday."

They walked along for a while in silence. Mike still felt uncomfortable thinking about Millie's past lover sleeping under her roof but the arrangement had been made and was nothing to do with him.

"Where has he been all this time while you've been bringing up his child?" Mike's tone was bitter. He wanted there to be no secrets between himself and Millie.

"He's been living in Amsterdam for the last six years. He had a child by his wife but now they are divorced and he has no access to his son. He is quite heartbroken about it and then he remembered he had a child in this country. He wants to be a good father to Lucy and to make up for the past. If he gives her a better life than I could have done I can't deny him that, now can I?"

"I suppose not. It's up to you, but I would have done everything I could have done for Lucy, you know. I'm reasonably well off and there would have been no more need for you to take in students, or to be a hairdresser, unless you liked it so much you wanted to carry on your business."

Millie put her arms round him and gave him a hug.

"I love you Mike Fairweather; did you know that?"

"I kind of guessed, but that's the first time you've told me."

"Is it, really?"

"Yes, really; and I don't mind hearing it again."

"Love you, love you, love you," said Millie, in between her kisses. A cheer went up from a passing boat, to Mike's embarrassment, and he gave them a wave. Millie laughed. It had been a wonderful afternoon. Hearing the noise Lucy ran back along the tow path.

"Were you two *kissing?*" she asked, with her face screwed up in an expression of disgust.

"There isn't a law against it, Lucy," said Millie, laughing.

"You should only kiss my Dad," said Lucy, angrily.

"Don't be silly, Lucy. I haven't seen your Dad for more than eight years; I don't even remember what he looks like now."

Lucy walked away, looking sulky, and kicked at the long grass at the side of the path. Mike felt as if the sun had gone behind the clouds and a storm was in the offing as they made their way home.

Beatrice and Ruth returned home from Chelsea with a car load of plants for the Japanese garden. Mike, who had gone back to get on with some work, watched them as they unloaded. Two huge azaleas were lifted out and humped through the house by Beatrice to be placed beside the teahouse. Ruth followed carrying a number of hollowed out pieces of bamboo, and returned for a box of hostas, and large ferns with pale green fronds. Mike wondered if Beatrice had been given some of the plants by the growers as she was well known as a horticulturist. They had certainly come back heavily laden with their booty.

"Had a good day?" he asked, as he walked down the winding path.

The women looked up in surprise. Beatrice continued sorting out the plants while Ruth took him to one side.

"We want to keep this garden, Mike. It's important to Beatrice. She's put so much effort into it and it means a lot to both of us."

"Of course you can keep it, but you realise that it goes with the house. You can't separate a garden from a house. We own it together. If you want the garden then you and your friend must buy the entire property, which means paying me half the asking price. You haven't any spare cash that I know of, so you will have to raise it some other way; perhaps with a bank loan or a mortgage. Talk it over with her."

"We have discussed it. Beatrice has a flat at Ealing. She thinks she can sell it for a good amount and then we could pay half the asking price and go on living here."

"It's time we saw a solicitor, I think, and sorted our affairs out. If you and Beatrice ever fell out Ruth, you might find things difficult, if she wanted to stay here and you were the one to find somewhere else to live."

"That's impossible. We shall always be here; it's you who will need to find somewhere else to live. It's intolerable for us having you living here."

Jan Pollard

"Living in my own house, you mean? Take care, Ruth, you're walking on eggshells. If you upset me I might put the house on the market and sell to the highest bidder, and I doubt if a flat in Ealing will meet such requirements. Just remember that this garden is going to be shown to millions of viewers when the programme goes out and people will be queuing up to buy it. Don't you ever forget that; and you, my dear Ruth, might find yourself last in the queue!"

CHAPTER 11

Linda was dressed for what she considered to be her film debut. She was wearing her favourite pink trousers from which her bottom bulged suggestively, leaving nothing to the imagination, and a purple blouse with a deep plunging neckline. A pair of purple high heeled sandals completed the picture. Her hair had been dyed a brassy blonde and she wore thick make up and dangling gold ear rings. Venus wondered what she looked like when she dressed less like a tart—probably very presentable, as her kindly nature showed in her face, despite the layers of cosmetics.

"What *does* she look like", grumbled Ed. "She's no Marilyn Monroe whatever she might think."

"She's all right," smiled Venus. "She's a decent sort underneath all that; she just got carried away a bit. If you don't do any close ups nobody will notice."

"Want to bet?" asked Ed, as he turned to give instructions to the film crew.

Ed had decided to continue with the filming before the gardens were completed. He wanted to show some of the residents working on the project to bring the programme to life. Linda's slab patio was finished at last and she had been taken to the nurseries to choose her terracotta pots and the plants to put in them. Beatrice had taken her round and they had chosen some pelargoniums of various colours, some bright red geraniums and some lilies. Beatrice had also suggested a hanging basket of fuchsias to give some extra interest. As the filming started Linda was shown potting her plants under Beatrice's instructions, as one of the work force fixed the hook on the wall for the hanging basket. When everything was finished two of the crew brought in a wooden garden seat and a tropical umbrella, which they placed into a heavy stand. Linda was overjoyed and behaved like a child who had just received a present from Father Christmas, kissing and thanking everybody including Beatrice, who looked none too pleased.

"I'd best get back to the launderette," said Linda, who wanted to relate her experiences to anybody who would listen. "Is it all right to go now?"

"Certainly; off you go," said Ed. "We've finished filming your little bit."

Linda tottered off down the road as fast as she could on her high heels, and removed the notice from the door of the launderette with a satisfied sigh. The notice had told her customers that due to filming the shop would be closed for the morning, and now she replaced it, rather regretfully, with one to say she was now open for business.

"Well, what did you think of *that*?" Ed asked, as they packed up, "nice to find someone so appreciative in this household."

"Don't speak too soon," said Venus, who had seen Malcolm approaching along the embankment. "Here comes trouble."

"Hey! I want a word with you," he shouted, pointing at Beatrice.

The film crew made a hasty departure, but Beatrice stood her ground and waited until he reached her.

"You've been trespassing; been in my greenhouse and taken my tools from my potting shed *and* used my watering can, without my permission. What have you got to say for yourself, eh?"

"I would have you know, Mr. Collins, that nobody was here to ask or I would have done so. As it was your son's plants were wilting, and would have been past recovery had they been left any longer. We are *both* gardeners, Mr. Collins, and you are a very good one. You'd have done the same yourself under similar circumstances."

Malcolm simmered down. The flattery had hit the mark, and he began to view Beatrice in a different light. She had actually *praised* his prowess as a gardener and it took an expert to acknowledge that.

"I would like to see how your vegetables are getting on, Mr. Collins, if you have the time to give me an escorted tour of your garden. Perhaps I can give you some tips to make it more colourful, if you have no objection. The viewers won't all be gardeners, and nobody knows which garden they'll choose. There'll be a silver cup and a certificate for the winner, you know."

Malcolm became only too anxious to co-operate. He wanted that silver cup badly, if only to boost his own self esteem, apart from which they would all buy him pints at the pub and tell him what a great chap he was; not that he didn't know that already of course.

"Mix up the type of leaves in a bed, curly kale, different types of lettuce, for example, and the fronds of carrots; think of yourself as an artist creating a colourful picture. Plant marrows and courgettes for their yellow flowers and put them near your runner beans, with their beautiful red blossoms. Edge your beds with beetroots, they have purple and dark green foliage and look splendid growing like that. There is no need to plant all your vegetables in straight lines, like your onions and broad beans here—oh, and talking about broad beans, did you know that putting nasturtiums near your broad beans can help to prevent them being attacked by black fly?"

Malcolm had never heard that before, but he was willing to give it a try.

"Nasturtiums are flowers, and this is a vegetable garden. That might go against me."

"Rubbish! They'll add to the colour. Plant them along the side fences, out of the way of your plots. You can eat the flowers in salads, you know. They did in Elizabethan days, and they're perfectly good to eat nowadays. The public like to be impressed and you've got to be the one to impress them, Mr. Collins."

Malcolm looked pleased as she left. Beatrice had made his day and he wondered why he had thought her a waste of space at their first meeting. She knew her onions. There was no doubt about that.

As Beatrice walked into Edna's garden she smiled to herself. She had won over the enemy. The only way to cope with a bully was to stand up to him, and she should know.

She wouldn't be where she was today if she had let people walk all over her. Being on the top of a situation was to be in charge of it, and Beatrice knew exactly how to do that.

William had nearly finished his planting and he had worked well. The healing garden was almost complete. The marigolds were already showing signs of coming into flower and the lavender would soon be out. There were a wide variety of plants, all planted in groups for different healing purposes; plants to heal wounds, or to encourage sleep, to reduce fever, to soothe skin complaints, or upset stomachs; even to ease headaches. The general public had a lot to learn about the plants the old monks had known, and had grown in their monastery gardens. She decided to make a chart for William about the plants he had put in the different beds and encourage him to talk about them. If he had the confidence to do so maybe she could persuade Ed to use that as a part of the programme. William's school might be interested to watch that episode if it was suggested to them as being educational. It would help to swell the number of viewers and William would become the hero of the hour.

With that in mind, Beatrice returned to the garden next door. Now she had a better relationship with Malcolm she might put the idea to him and see what he thought of it. Malcolm welcomed her back as if she was an old friend and agreed with everything she suggested. As it was half term William was around somewhere and once he put in an appearance Malcolm promised to send him along the terrace to find her, then she could discuss it with him.

Beatrice returned home and put in a call to Ed. He considered it to be a good idea and was amazed to hear that she had calmed Malcolm down and that all was well as far as his garden was concerned.

"Do you think we might offer him a cordoned apple tree along his fence? It would look good and the way to do it would almost make a programme on its own plus the rest of his garden, and the new ideas I've just suggested to him."

"You mean he's agreed to something you suggested! You're amazing, Beatrice."

"Oh, it's nothing. You only have to throw your weight about a bit and things soon fall into place."

It was hard to imagine Beatrice, for all her large size, crushing Malcolm. It was enough to make the mind boggle.

"So he's just a big pussy cat now is he?"

"I wouldn't say that exactly, but I can manage him."

"Well we'll leave him to you in future. Perhaps you'd like to go and see him now he's at home and tell him about the apple tree; a present for a good boy! I'll get the nursery to deliver one right away and we'll incorporate it into the afternoon's filming."

Beatrice guffawed with laughter, making Mike miss out a vital part of his accounting. If he had known what a mess of his life this woman was going to make he would never have agreed to take part in the garden scheme. Even falling in love with Millie had turned out to have its problems.

There was a knock at the back door and Beatrice answered it.

"Hello, William. I hoped you'd find me. I want to discuss the plants in your garden with you."

"Dad, said."

"Put you on the telly. It'll be nice to have a decent programme on there for a change."

The door slammed behind her and Beatrice went to tell Malcolm the good news about the apple tree. She would be his friend for life now.

Mike sighed and got down to putting his accounts in order. Why did that wretched woman have to be so noisy; there was no getting away from Beatrice.

Jan Pollard

The next session of filming went well with Malcolm planting his cordon apple tree and talking about his plans for the vegetable garden.

"I'm thinking about it as an artist would of his painting," said Malcolm, proudly, as if it was all his own idea. "Colours and—."

"Textures?" suggested Beatrice.

"Exactly; textures," said Malcolm, beaming at her. "Crinkly leaves amongst smooth leaves and different colours of greens; and I've planted nasturtiums along the fence. They keep down the black fly, which you might not have known about. That's a tip we gardeners know."

Beatrice gave him a hard look. He had been an apt pupil but she was not too pleased to find her conversation with him relayed as if it was all his own idea. Ed was astounded at his co-operation. Beatrice had worked wonders. Malcolm accompanied the film crew into Edna's garden to encourage William to speak to the camera about his work, but his presence only served to make William more nervous.

"We'll leave that part until William feels a bit more confident," said Ed, "and go on to start filming the willow arbour at Number 2 if the child there is at home and Beatrice can show her how it's done. I don't like to waste an opportunity while she's on half term holiday. Once she knows how to do the weaving we can come back later when some progress has been made."

The withes had been delivered and lay in a pile at the top of Millie's garden. Lucy was called to see how the shape of the arbour was formed while the men of the ground force pushed them into the grass in a circle. Under instruction from Beatrice the men began to weave the branches in and out along the initial structure until a few rows had been completed.

"Can you see how it's done?" asked Beatrice. Lucy nodded. "Then you come and try. All these branches will grow leaves and knit together until you have your own leafy arbour. You can sit inside and read like the statue of the little girl here."

"She's sitting on the top of a pillar," said Lucy. "That's different."

The Hidden Gardens

"I stand corrected," said Beatrice sweetly, bearing in mind that the camera was on her and it was best not to show how annoying she found this child.

Lucy made an effort but found the withes too strong to bend, apart from which they scratched her hands.

"We'll have to get the ground force to finish it if it's too much for her, but we've got a bit of film which is what really matters," said Ed. "Perhaps later we can get her mother to be filmed giving her a hand; make it a family activity."

"My Dad will be here to-morrow," said Lucy. "He'll help me to do it."

"That's marvellous! We'll film you all together. Ask your mother if it's convenient for us to come tomorrow and we'll have a session filming here. We still have to plant the silver birch trees in the corner and possibly a buddleia beside the arbour; that's sometimes called the butterfly bush because of all the different butterflies it attracts. I'm sure you'd like one of those."

"Yes, I would. I'll just go and ask Mum."

Millie had cancelled her appointments the next day because Lucy's father was coming.

She was anxious that this meeting should go as smoothly as possible, and maybe the film activity would help to break the ice, so filming was arranged for the following day, after the ground force had installed the solar fountain in the centre of Edna's pool.

Guy had been waiting for them at Number 8 for what had seemed hours. He carefully avoided eye contact with Gerry as he and his team assembled the large pieces of the fountain and fixed the water mechanism, and was transfixed by the sight of the water bubbling through the centre fount and splashing over the sides into the recess beneath. As it flooded through the channels it brought the brilliant blue mosaic tiles to life and reflected the box trees on its surface. The whole team were delighted with the result; it was magical and turned the garden into a virtual paradise.

"How about using two of those enormous blue pots you are about to take round to Number 2?" suggested Venus. "Four of them will never fit under her pergola; they are much too big, and they would look just right on the blue tiled area in front of this house."

"Splendid idea!" agreed Beatrice, "I was just thinking that myself. Filled with pink and white rhododendrons they would finish off this garden perfectly. I can't imagine Millie Carrington would object. It would leave her a bit more money to spend on her own garden. A few hollyhocks and foxgloves wouldn't come amiss along the side fences of her rose garden. Those roses won't give colour all the summer."

"I'll ask her about it," said Venus. "I'm sure she won't mind."

With Gerry in tow Venus called on Millie who made no objection to two of her enormous pots being transferred to the garden at Number 8. In fact Millie now showed little interest in what happened to her garden after being so keen on the idea at first. Venus wondered if it had anything to do with the arrival of Lucy's father. Millie looked very miserable as if something was troubling her, but perhaps it had nothing to do with that.

Guy sat in the gazebo sipping a glass of wine, and watched the water running through the blue tiled channels. It was so beautiful. Guy appreciated beauty in all its shapes and forms, both human and abstract. Gerry had done a superb job putting all this together. He and his workers only had the barbecue area in Venus and Benji's garden to complete and then he would be finished. The other two men would replace the back fences to the properties after the filming was finished, and the public had been given access to the gardens.

Guy would have left before that took place. Next week he and Gerry would be in Morocco and Damian would be left to enjoy all this beauty on his own. Guy comforted himself with the thought that he had helped to make this garden for Damian's pleasure. Damian would never have been able to do all the digging and the planting as he disliked manual work and the tedious business of fitting the mosaic tiles together would have driven him crazy. It eased Guy's conscience slightly to think of all the work he had put into the project and he lifted up his glass of wine and made a toast, to old friends and new. He leaned back on the white wrought iron seat, which he found uncomfortable, and decided that if the sky was clear that night he would sit here with Damian and look at the stars through the open sides of the gazebo. They would listen to their tape of the nightingales singing as they drank their wine and watch the water splashing gently over the sides of the Moorish fountain. It would be sheer bliss, and Damian would be happy. Guy closed his mind to the ugly reality of what next week would bring and smiled contentedly.

Filming was over for the day and Beatrice returned to Ruth's garden. She had gleaned a bit of information which she intended to take back to Ruth. The child's father was coming the next day, which might make a difference to Mike's relationship with her mother. If the father stayed with Millie then Mike would have to live elsewhere and hopefully move out of their lives altogether. That would suit Beatrice who wanted to live in domestic bliss with Ruth without Mike on the doorstep. She had already created a high bamboo fence between the gardens, and had planted japonica and Japanese ivy, with its spectacular crimson autumn leaves, to spread over the fencing on the other side. Two cut leafed maple trees would shield the back of the tea house from view, at the end of the garden. Apart from the occasional noise from the trains as they clattered along the line at the back, they would live in a Japanese paradise.

There was still so much to do. The hollowed out bamboo had to be placed to form a waterfall, one piece carefully arranged above the other to tip the water into the next, as it flowed into the goldfish pool. It had to be exact to create the right feel to the garden and Beatrice worked assiduously to get it to her satisfaction. A trickling stream of water ran over the rocks and into the bamboo waterfall before it finished in the pool. All she needed now, apart from some fat goldfish, was a small Japanese bridge to cross the pool, and two carved stone lanterns to make it look authentic. Tomorrow morning she would take Ruth to find what they wanted, and maybe they would go out to lunch. The pleasure of being in her lover's company would outweigh the embarrassment of being part of the afternoon's filming, when Millie Carrington would be there.

Jan Pollard

Beatrice looked at the carpet of moss covering the garden on either side of the stream and at the flowering cherry she had placed so carefully on the opposite side to the azaleas, and felt well pleased with herself. The creeping thyme and the lichens would soon start growing up the carefully placed stones to give a feeling of age.

One day soon she and Ruth would take the winding stepping stone path, walk across the little bridge and step behind the screen of bamboo and enter the teahouse. There they would make their vows of everlasting love over a cup of green tea and meditate on life. The thought of the happy days to come gave Beatrice a feeling of great satisfaction. It was all she had ever wanted from life; a perfect Japanese garden and someone who shared her obsession, and whom she could subject to her will.

CHAPTER 12

The following morning when Millie opened her front door she was shocked by the appearance of Lucy's father. Ian Francis had always been a slim man but the man on her front door step looked different; haggard and dirty, as if he had been sleeping rough.

His eyes had a hunted, shifty look, as he glanced up and down the terrace before going into the hall. His hair was thin and wispy and his moustache drooped, giving him the appearance of having just walked off the set of a cowboy film. His face was much thinner making his nose long and pinched like that of a rat.

Millie was unimpressed. He still bore a faint resemblance to the youth she had set up home with years ago; full of bravado, but a coward at heart. How she had ever considered herself to be in love with him was mystery to her. She must have been pretty desperate to leave home and live with him; a teenage urge for independence she imagined, as her parents had not liked him.

"Hallo, Millie. Good of you to let me stay. Where's the kid?"

"She's in the garden at the moment; she'll be in shortly. We didn't expect you quite so soon; I'll put on the kettle."

"A cuppa would be nice. I'm parched; been travelling for days."

"Where did you come from? Amsterdam? I thought that was a fairly easy journey."

"Not the way I came."

"And what way was that, by 'plane?"

"No, not exactly."

Ian seemed not to want to talk about his journey and sat drinking tea until the pot ran dry. Millie was puzzled. Where was the man who had promised to do so much for Lucy? This man looked uncomfortable, as if something was troubling him and she regretted her offer to put him up for the week, but she was hardly able to turn him out just as he had arrived. He slumped in the chair as if he was exhausted.

"How long have you been in Amsterdam, Ian?"

"Six years, I suppose, off and on. I'm in the import and export business so I travelled around quite a bit."

"Did that include England?"

"Occasionally, but I never stayed long."

There was something strange about the whole situation, thought Millie, who was determined to get to the bottom of it. Why should he have suddenly come back into her life if he had already returned to this country on other occasions since Lucy had been born?

"Why didn't you come to see us before? I don't understand that. You knew we might be here. You came to this house enough times while my parents were alive."

"I didn't try to find you, Millie, because I had a wife in Amsterdam. It could have complicated things for me. She was a jealous woman and now she's left me and taken my son. They've simply disappeared. Can you imagine how I felt about that?"

"Only too well; you disappeared once out of my life—remember?"

Ian looked uncomfortable.

"Don't rub it in, Millie. I feel bad about it. You've turned into a lovely woman. The skinny little girl I once knew has developed quite a figure. I hardly recognised you."

"I don't want your compliments, Ian. You can keep them to yourself."

"Is there another man in your life, now? I can't imagine you're alone after all these years, a gorgeous looking woman like you."

"It's none of your business. You came here to see Lucy, not to see me. I only agreed to this because I thought you were going to help Lucy financially, but it doesn't look as if you have any money to your name by the look of you."

"I've plenty stashed away. I'll see she never wants for anything once the insurance company pays out."

"What's that supposed to mean? What insurance money?"

"It's just a matter of time; there's nothing to worry about; I've got it all in hand; now where's this daughter of mine?"

"Lucy's in her secret garden, behind the trellis at the top. She's excited about seeing you, so take things gently won't you."

Millie let him go and find Lucy on his own and followed behind. Watching as Lucy ran into her father's open arms distressed her, as Lucy hugged and kissed him. He had no right to her affection and she blamed herself for agreeing to his coming. His arrival would make a difference to her setting up home with Mike and the three of them becoming one happy family. Lucy would never love Mike the same way now she had found her real father and Millie wanted everything to be perfect with Mike; so perfect that she had put Lucy's happiness before her own.

"So I have a real little princess for a daughter," said Ian. "One I never knew anything about until now. You look just like your mother Lucy. I'd have known you anywhere."

Lucy was all smiles.

"Now you're here, Dad, you'll help me with my willow arbour, won't you. I'm finding it very hard to weave these sticks in and out. My hands aren't big enough."

"Of course I will, my princess. Just show me what to do."

Millie joined in and they managed another two courses before the film crew came through the side gate. Seeing the family busy at work in such a natural way Ed signed to the crew to be quiet and to begin filming. After a while the camera man drew closer and closer to the group until Ian, looking up, realised they were not alone.

Jan Pollard

"What's this? What's going on?"

"They're filming us for a television programme, Dad. Isn't it exciting! Now you'll be on it as well."

But Ian had gone. Pushing the camera man to one side he had sprinted down the path and gone into the house, slamming the back door behind him.

"Nervous is he?" asked Ed, surprised at Ian's sudden departure.

Mille shook her head. "I've no idea. I haven't seen him for years. He came to see Lucy. He didn't know about the filming this morning. I hadn't got round to telling him."

"Well, not to worry. We've got a bit of film with you all busily working away, but I'll ask the ground force to finish off your arbour for you Lucy. We're setting up the large barbecue today at Number 6 now the platform is finished but they'll have a bit of time to spare to finish your arbour. Perhaps you can help your Mum to plant her clematis instead."

Lucy shook her head. "My Dad's here, so I can't—sorry."

Ed smiled. "That's O.K. We'll move on to Number 6 and film the barbecue being put into position. Fixing that and getting it working will take most of the morning."

Millie was angry, and puzzled. She returned to the house to find Ian listening to the World Service on the radio. Lucy was showing him how her play station worked but she might as well have been talking to a brick wall for all the notice he was taking of his daughter. It was going to be a long week if he intended to stay indoors all the time, for reasons best known to him.

That night Millie prepared a meal for her unwelcome guest, who joined them in the kitchen. Lucy was still enamoured of her father and chatted away to him ceaselessly.

"How long is this garden project going on?" Ian asked.

"I think it's nearly finished, Dad. There won't be any more to film in Mum's garden now she's planted the big blue pots."

"The garden opening won't be until June," said Millie. "You won't be around then I hope; in fact I want you to go next week. The students will want their room soon and I have to get it prepared."

Lucy grew angry. "Why does Dad have to go so soon? I want him to stay for always."

"What a kind girl you are, princess. I shall be gone before your garden is open, I'm afraid."

"You've got a big bed, Mum. Dad could share that."

"That's enough of that, Lucy. Your Dad's not staying, and that's definite."

Ian patted his daughter's hand, and smiled at her. He remembered the Millie of old and the thought of sharing her bed brought back some pleasant memories of hot, steamy nights of sexual activity.

"We had some good times together, didn't we, Millie. A right little raver you were in those days."

"What's that?" asked Lucy.

Millie pushed her chair back quickly and began to clear the table.

"If you want to talk like that in front of your daughter you can leave now. The past is the past and the present only concerns me. You chose not to be a part of it and I've made my own life, with Lucy."

"Anyone would think you'd taken the veil to hear you speak but I know you better than that," said Ian, giving her a knowing look.

Millie felt like slapping his face. She had been taken in completely by him and now it was too late.

"The Simpsons are on the telly, Lucy; you won't want to miss that, will you. Perhaps your Dad will take you out somewhere to-morrow so he can get to know you better. That's what he's come here for; or so he says."

"Will you take me to Regent's Park Zoo, Dad? It isn't far from here but Mum could never afford to take me."

Ian glared at Millie. "Surely you could have managed that! All kids love the Zoo."

"Well I don't. You can take her if she wants to go."

"I will if you give me the money."

"What! You haven't even got enough for that! Some fortune you're going to spend on her! I'd forgotten what you're like, Ian;

you're no good to anyone. I think you'd better leave the day after to-morrow. I don't want you here."

Ian gave her a dirty look. If that was how she felt he'd give her a taste of her own medicine before he left.

"Please, Mum," wheedled Lucy, "please."

"Well, just this once then." Millie got out her purse and handed Lucy two twenty pound notes.

"You take care of them, Lucy. The treat is for you, not your Dad."

Ian spent the evening fiddling with the radio to get the news on the World Service until it was time for Lucy to go to bed.

"Goodnight, my princess. See you in the morning."

It sickened Millie to see Lucy hugging and kissing him goodnight. He was just the same as he had always been; conning his way into people's affections and helping himself to their money. The sooner he left the better.

She went to bed early and wedged a chair under the door handle for her own safety. At least she would hear him if he tried to come into her bedroom. She stayed awake until the early hours of the morning and then fell asleep with exhaustion.

Breakfast was taken in silence apart from Lucy's excited chatter, and it was a relief when they had left the house. Ian seemed to be less nervous about being seen in public with Lucy hanging onto his arm. It was highly unlikely that anyone would be looking for him in Regent's Park Zoo, especially with his young daughter around.

Once they had gone Millie telephoned Mike. Ruth and Beatrice had left for their day's shopping trip to choose the bridge and the lanterns for the Japanese garden. Millie had seen them getting into the station wagon as Lucy had left with her father so she knew it was safe to speak to him. Mike came round immediately and held her tightly within the safety of his arms.

"I'm frightened of him, Mike; the way he looks at me sometimes scares me. I've told him to leave to-morrow, but I'm afraid he won't go. It's another week before the students come back and he knows that so I'm afraid he'll hang around until then."

Mike kissed her, tenderly. "I don't like this, my darling. Let me tell him to go. I'll hustle him off the premises."

"Lucy thinks he's wonderful. If she sees you doing that she'll hate you for it, and I want the three of us to be one happy family, more than anything in the world."

"And so we shall be, my love, very soon now. Ruth has seen her solicitor and has agreed to everything. Once Ruth has left for school on the last day of term I shall move in with you, and we can either stay here or move to another house, if that's what you would like. I don't care where we live as long as we are together."

"Darling, Mike. I want you in my life, so much."

Mike held her close and kissed her passionately. They were both aroused and he began to lead her upstairs to her bedroom, when they heard a knock at the back door.

"Send them away, for pity's sake. I've been waiting for this moment when we can be alone together without Lucy around."

Millie ran downstairs and Mike heard her speaking to a woman whom she ushered into her salon.

"You haven't got a customer, have you? At this time of all times! I can't believe it, Millie."

"I'd forgotten she was coming in the heat of the moment; oh, Mike, I wanted you so much. Forgive me darling, please forgive me. Come back at mid-day. I should be finished with this blow dry by then, although I have two other customers this afternoon."

Mike kissed her briefly and returned home to deal with his accounting, simmering with rage and frustration.

Millie telephoned him when her customer had left and prepared them a light lunch which Mike found difficult to eat, and Millie only picked at her food.

"I want to wait, Mike, until we can relax together. I don't know when Ian is bringing Lucy home and I shall be on edge all the time. I don't want a few moments of sexual satisfaction; I want it to mean something between us. I've never had it like that before. I love you so much, Mike, I want it to be perfect."

"It will be, sweetheart, as perfect as I can make it; just try me." Mike took her hands in his and tried to persuade her to go upstairs with him, but she was unwilling and he decided he was being unfair and left her alone.

"I'm afraid of Ian, Mike. I can't get him out of my mind. He could be violent at times in the past."

"He didn't try anything last night, did he? My God! I'll kill him if he comes anywhere near you."

"No. I put a chair under the handle of my door to keep him out, but I don't think he tried. I stayed awake for most of the night, I was so nervous."

"When he's gone to bed to-night my darling, switch your light off and on and leave your front door unlocked. I'll stay awake all night. I'm on the other side of the wall remember, so shout if you need me and I'll soon deal with him."

"Dear Mike. It seems too much to ask."

"Why should it be? Your safety is all important to me. When I share your bed, Millie, you'll never have anything to worry about again."

"Only you," said Millie, giving him a peck on his cheek, and smiling.

Mike caught her round her waist and pulled her onto his lap. He undid her blouse and held the creamy white breasts he had so longed to fondle. Millie shifted her weight so she sat astride his legs and nestled his head against her bosom, as he ran his tongue across her raspberry pink nipples.

"You're a tease, Millie Carrington."

"Good things are worth waiting for, didn't you know?"

Mike groaned. "God, woman; I'm only human. Stop playing around with my feelings Millie. I want you now!"

There was yet another knock on the door and another customer had arrived.

"That's why we can't go any further," said Millie, as she prepared to let the woman in. "Today is my busy day; too busy to make love, my darling."

The Hidden Gardens

Mike decided there and then that he would insist on her giving up her hairdressing once he went to live with her. Hairdressing and making love were totally incompatible.

The visit to the Zoo had not been a success. Like so many things that were eagerly anticipated it had failed to live up to Lucy's expectations. Her father had decided to stay inside the monkey house rather than stand and watch their antics outside, and he seemed to prefer to stay and look at the reptiles inside a darkened tunnel rather than go to see the elephants despite Lucy's constant requests. Even an ice cream was refused as, according to her father, the price was astronomical. Lucy felt sure the price of the admission tickets had left some money over, which her father had put into his own pocket.

That evening Lucy was so quiet that Millie felt things must have gone badly, and she was secretly glad. There were no references to his 'little princess' and Lucy seemed glad to spend her time up in her bedroom listening to her tapes which was unusual. She called down that she was going to bed as she felt tired, without coming down to say goodnight to her father.

"Didn't she enjoy it?" asked Millie.

Ian shrugged. "Nothing seemed right for her today."

"That's not like, Lucy. She loves outings as a rule."

"Well she didn't love this one."

Ian went back to fiddling with the radio leaving Millie to wonder what it was he was so keen to find out. Maybe it was something to do with his murky past and she feared she might be harbouring a criminal under her roof.

"You're going to-morrow, don't forget, Ian. Getting to know your daughter hasn't worked out and I don't want you here. You came under false pretences it would seem, although for what reason I'd rather not know, but I want you to leave—understand."

Ian, who was holding the radio to his ear as the transmission was weak didn't bother to reply. About midnight Millie went to bed and heard Ian come up the stairs soon after. She switched her light off and on and heard Mike knock on his side of the wall

Jan Pollard

in reply. There would be no need to jam the chair under the door handle to-night. Mike was close by and she felt safe enough to fall asleep.

She awoke to find someone in bed with her, and hands touching her body. Thinking in her half wakefulness that it was Mike she rolled towards him only to feel her arms pinned to her sides and a tongue pushed roughly into her mouth, and she woke to the frightening realisation that it was Ian who was attempting to rape her.

Millie struggled and tried to scream as he held her down, but it was not until she managed to knee him in the groin that his shout of pain alerted Mike. He was in the house and up the stairs two at a time and pulled Ian off Millie's bed, while punching him hard on the chin. Ian reeled backwards, stunned by the appearance of this stranger, only to receive another punch on his nose. Blood was pouring down his face as he staggered to the bathroom, pushing Lucy to one side as she ran into her mother's bedroom.

To Lucy's amazement her mother was being comforted by Mr Fairweather. What was he doing in their house when he lived next door? It was all most puzzling, especially as he seemed to have been fighting with her father.

"Get him out, Mike; for God's sake, get rid of him," wept Millie.

"Look after your mother, Lucy. I've got a job to do."

Lucy sat on the bed with her arms round Millie, feeling very frightened.

"What's wrong, Mum? What's Mr Fairweather doing here?"

"It's your father, Lucy. I should never have let him come here. He doesn't want to help us at all; he only came just to help himself." Millie wiped her eyes and blew her nose, feeling a little more in control of the situation. "I asked Mike to stay awake on his side of the wall because I was afraid of being here alone with your Dad."

Lucy was shocked. "Did he hurt you, Mum?"

"Not really dear. Mike made sure of that."

There was a scuffling noise on the staircase as Mike booted Ian out, throwing his suitcase after him.

The Hidden Gardens

"Clear off, you scum! You're not wanted here."

Ian finished pulling on his trousers in the garden and made his escape along the embankment. It had been like a nightmare. He had no idea of the identity of the man who had appeared from nowhere, giving him a bloody nose. Millie must have a lover who had turned up just in time to prevent him from raping her, and yet she had seemed to welcome his attentions at first.

He would have to hole up elsewhere until the Dutch police gave up their search for his whereabouts. Now he had no access to the World Service he would never know if they had found the remains of his wife, whom he had murdered for her insurance money. He had been a fool to have messed about with Millie, but seeing her as she looked now had awoken all the sexual feelings he had once felt for her. They had spent some wild nights together in the past before she had fallen for the kid and decided to keep the baby. That had spoilt everything.

"I didn't like my Dad," said Lucy, snuggling into her mother's bed. "He wouldn't let me have an ice cream at the Zoo; he said they were too expensive."

"Really, well I expect they were, but you could have bought one for yourself. I gave you enough money."

"Dad took it. He took all of it."

Millie made no reply. It sounded just like Ian, to steal from his own child. Lucy had learned the hard way that people are not always what they seem. His denial of a simple thing like an ice cream had turned the situation around. Mike had come to her rescue and Lucy would never forget that. The possibility of things going well from now on filled her with happiness, and she closed her eyes and slept.

Mike put his head round the door to say he was leaving and saw they were both asleep. Two blonde heads nestled together on the pillow, so alike they looked more like sisters than mother and daughter. He closed the door quietly and let himself out, to return to the house where he was no longer wanted.

Only a few weeks left now and he would have a family to call his own.

CHAPTER 13

Damian parked the almost new silver Audi outside Number 8 and got out of the driving seat to admire it. His mother's heavy chiffonier and the delicate French writing desk with its marquetry work in ivory had sold for high prices in the sale room. He ought to have disposed of the chiffonier long ago. It was much too big for his little house, but it had been a wrench to see the writing desk going under the hammer. He had always liked it and hated parting with it but if he was to buy a decent car for Guy he knew it would have to be sold. He flicked a duster over the already highly polished exterior, gave it one last satisfied look and went indoors to find Guy.

To his surprise Guy was nowhere to be seen. Damian walked up the garden to the gazebo but Guy was not there either. He was usually at home at this time of the day preparing their evening meal before going to the club for the evening. It was odd. The house was strangely silent and Damian began to feel that something was wrong.

On the kitchen table he found an unopened bottle of his favourite red wine with a letter propped up against it addressed to himself. Damian tore open the envelope and scanned the contents. Guy had gone. At first he could scarcely take it in and then, after the initial shock, he read it more carefully. Guy had left the Gay Club and would be en route for Morocco by the time Damian read his letter, and what was worse, he had gone off with Gerry Finch. Damian's worst fears had been realised. If he had only refused to be a part of the garden scheme this would never have happened. Now he realised why Guy had been so cool towards him of late. There was someone else in his life.

Damian sank onto one of the kitchen chairs, put his head in his hands and howled. The sound was like an animal's cry of pain. The sacrifice he had made to buy Guy a classic car which he knew he would have loved, was all in vain. He had paid a terrible price to have a wonderful garden. He had lost the one person who meant more to him than anyone in the world. Damian sobbed and sobbed without caring who heard him.

Linda was watering the flowers on her patio when she heard a terrible noise coming from next door. Someone was weeping, loudly. The noise went on and on and Linda decided to investigate. She put down her watering can and made her way across the back of their garden and into the one next door. The sound appeared to be coming from the kitchen so she peered in through the window, where she could see Damian slumped across the table in a state of terrible distress. Linda, who was a kind soul, immediately went into the kitchen to do what she could to help.

"Whatever has happened, Mr Wentworth? Is there anything I can do?"

Damian looked up to see who it was, and then slumped down again.

"It's Guy," he sobbed. "He's gone."

"He's dead, you mean?" asked Linda, who could think of no other reason for such an outburst of sorrow.

"He might as well be," moaned Damian. "He's left me. All he left was a note. I shall never see him again."

Linda was sympathetic. She knew how she had felt when their Alice had cleared off and left a note. It had broken her heart. It seemed strange that her neighbour should feel the same about losing his partner but it couldn't be as bad as losing your own flesh and blood, could it?

Jan Pollard

Linda patted his hand. "I felt just the same when our Alice went without telling us where she was going, but I just keep hoping she'll come back one day. Hoping keeps you going, you know. You mustn't give in to it; you'll make yourself ill."

"You're right, Mrs Collins. I must pull myself together. But there's no hope of him coming back, none at all."

"I'm so sorry. Look I'll put the kettle on and make you a nice cup of tea. You'll feel a lot better after that."

Linda looked around the kitchen where everything was kept in its place and soon found the kettle and a tray on which she put two mugs, the milk and the sugar. As she poured the water into the pot she noticed that Damian had lifted his head off the table and was sitting with his head bowed, looking the soul of misery.

Linda handed him a mug of tea. "Come on, Mr Wentworth, drink up. There's nothing like a cup of tea when the world seems to have come to an end. I'll join you, if I may."

Damian nodded. "You're very kind, Mrs Collins."

"Please call me Linda; I much prefer it. Mrs Collins sounds so stuffy and I'm not at all stuffy; just the opposite in fact."

"You're good to stay. I felt like ..."

"Now don't talk like that. Things will be different I've no doubt, and there'll be times when you feel lonely, but there's no need. I'm just next door, and I'll always come round if you feel like a chat. I hardly ever see Malcolm. He's either working, in the garden, or down at the pub. He only comes in for his meals or to watch the football and William is never at home these days. The only people I get to talk to are at the launderette. I'd be very lonely otherwise, so I'd be very pleased to come round, if you'd like me to, at any time."

Damian looked at her. She had a kind, motherly face even if it was smothered with some kind of pancake make up. He realised she was genuinely trying to help him and he was grateful.

"You're a good person, Linda. Thank you for coming round."

Linda smiled and put the things into the sink to wash up later, the way she did at home.

The Hidden Gardens

"I'd better go and put the car in the garage," said Damian. "I don't want to leave it on the street. I've rented one round the back, next to the Fairweather's garage."

"Is it new?" asked Linda, who had no idea that Damian possessed a car.

"Almost; I bought it to-day, for Guy, but he won't need it now."

Linda was shocked. No wonder he was so upset. That Guy should be ashamed of himself treating such a kind man so heartlessly.

"Well, now you can have it for yourself, and enjoy driving about in it. Your friend didn't deserve such a wonderful present going away and leaving you like that."

Linda was full of righteous indignation but her words only served to bring on another storm of weeping.

"Oh, dear, dear, dear, I didn't mean to upset you, perhaps I'd better go and leave you on your own. *Please* don't do anything silly; it'll all come out in the wash, you'll see. Time is a great healer—."

Linda felt as if she was making the situation worse although she had no idea why that should be, as she felt genuinely sorry for her poor neighbour.

As she left she assured him that she would return after work the next day to see if he was feeling better and Damian raised his hand in acknowledgement without looking at her. Every day after she had closed the launderette, Linda popped round next door. She brought a small gift of food each time which she had bought at the supermarket in the parade; something Damian could cook for himself, which were mostly items in tins. Damian was grateful and offered to pay, although most of the things she bought were not to his taste. Guy had cooked delicate dishes which often needed considerable preparation as Guy had a preference for expensive food. Damian had left it to him to choose what they ate as Guy enjoyed cooking. Now Guy had left he realised how spoilt he had been and he often resorted to eating out as it saved a lot of bother.

Jan Pollard

He was deeply grateful to Linda. She cared about his well being and always appeared with a smile of encouragement on her face, anxious to see that he never lapsed into a terrible depression again. She had even suggested that he found himself another friend, or looked for a woman to share his life. Damian had laughed, shortly, at that suggestion.

"You'll be getting me fixed up with Edna, Linda, before you've finished."

They had both laughed at that.

"You see, you're getting better," said Linda.

"I thought I'd never find anything to laugh about again," admitted Damian. "You're a wonderful woman, Linda. You've done me a power of good."

Linda was pleased. "No-one's ever called me that before, and I'm glad I've been able to help you, Mr Wentworth. We're put on this earth to help other people, or so I believe."

Damian gave her a searching look. She was a treasure and one her wretched husband had never appreciated, and more than anything he wanted to do something for her. She had been there for him when he most needed help and she was there with her smiling face every time he got back from Westminster. He never wanted to lose her. Both his mother and Guy had rejected him most cruelly. Linda would never be unkind to anyone; a loyal friend who would always be there, in the background.

"I hope you don't think me presumptuous, Linda, but would you like to work for me? It's only a suggestion. I know you already have your job at the launderette and you might not want to give that up, but I would give you a proper wage and you could still look after your own family, as you're next door. What do you think?"

Linda was flabbergasted. She had thought she would have to stay at the launderette until she drew her pension. Life would be so much more pleasant working next door.

"I'll have to ask Malcolm, of course, but I'd really like a job like that. I'd have more time for my little garden."

"Good. I'm glad you like the idea of being my housekeeper. Let me know how your husband feels about it."

The Hidden Gardens

"I will; and thank you Mr Wentworth."

"Not at all; I think we'll get along really well together, don't you?"

Linda left all smiles. She could see no reason why Malcolm should object, especially as she would earn a decent wage for working fewer hours. At the launderette she only earned peanuts.

Malcolm laughed when she told him.

"His fancy boy's left him has he; so the next best thing is you, is it Linda?"

"That's crude Malcolm, really horrible. You know he doesn't fancy me, as you put it. He isn't that sort. He's a really kind gentleman, and that's something you'll never be. He treats me properly, and I shall enjoy being his housekeeper."

"I'm only joking, Linda. Keep your hair on. If you think it'll work out then take the job. As long as you can look after us as well I can't see anything wrong with it."

Linda was relieved. Having to ask Malcolm for his opinion about everything annoyed her but it made life easier in the long run, and Linda was all for an easy life. Now Alice had left and taken her problems with her things were a lot quieter at home.

That week she received a letter from the owners of the launderette to say it had been sold to a bank who wanted to open a small branch in the suburbs. Linda thanked her lucky stars for the opportunity to continue working which had come her way. Fewer and fewer people were using the launderette since the area had been developed into upmarket properties, mostly for people who worked in the city. The large Edwardian houses on the other side of the park had been turned into flats, and most people had washing machines these days. Linda had seen the demise of the launderette coming for some time but had put it to the back of her mind. It was no good worrying about things until they happened, and now it had happened it had come at exactly the right time.

That evening she explained it all to Mr Wentworth who said that it was meant to be, and arranged for her to start working for him almost immediately. The owners of the launderette gave her a larger pay packet than usual when she left—not exactly a

Jan Pollard

golden handshake, as she explained to Malcolm later, but more like enough to buy a few packets of soapflakes. Malcolm was indignant and wanted Linda to make a fuss about it, but that was not Linda's way. She was too happy about her new job to bother, and Malcolm could go on about it as much as he liked. Linda ignored him. Malcolm always had to find *something* to moan about.

Everyone in the terrace had received a letter from the television company to tell them the first programme of 'Looking at your Backyard' was being shown on Channel 4 that evening. Although there was still some filming to be completed, that would be finished before the end of the series. There was great excitement as all the residents, apart from Edna, settled down to look at the first of the seven programmes.

Venus had considered asking Edna to come and see it with her, but decided against it. This first programme would show the ground being cleared, and Edna would see her old pram being shunted into the skip with all the rest of her rubbish and that might upset her.

Beatrice and Ruth were making a recording of all the programmes so Mike decided to do his viewing later, when they were out of the house. Ruth had come into the kitchen while he was eating his lonely evening meal to ask him to join them but he had declined. Seeing the two of them sitting together on the sofa in such close proximity was too much to bear. He decided to make a copy to give to Millie at a later date. At least Ruth was trying her best not to upset him in any way while the arrangements for the sale of the house were being worked out. His meals were left for him to warm up in the microwave, and his bed linen was laundered as well as his shirts. He had no complaints as long as they left him alone and kept themselves to themselves.

Damian had switched on the television to watch the programme, and was impressed by the introduction. Ed had employed a helicopter firm to take a view of the terrace gardens from the air. They looked like a jumble of trees and poor ill kempt lawns, apart from his garden which Guy had looked after so carefully. The gazebo looked splendid from above and the

The Hidden Gardens

lawn had been mown to perfection. Damian felt a sense of pride as he looked at his plot and compared it to the others. Suddenly the view changed to show Gerry and his work force removing the back fences and working with a rotovator to clear away the old soil. Damian felt like shouting at him and got up to switch off the programme. The man looked like one of those muscular Chippendales he had once seen in a show at the club; all brawn and massive pectorals. No wonder Guy had found him attractive if all he was looking for had been sex. Damian had thought Guy wanted more than that out of a relationship, which was why they had got on so well. He must have been wrong about Guy. He would finish with that side of his life now Guy had gone, and live quietly on his own. He had made one mistake and never intended to make another one like that.

Malcolm watched the programme, avidly. He saw the work force taking down his old potting shed and throwing it into the skip with all of Edna's rubbish. It made him grind his teeth in rage. How dare they do that without his permission! He had loved his beloved old potting shed and every spider and cobweb inside it. He had spent hours sitting on a box in the doorway smoking a cigarette and contemplating his vegetables, willing them to grow. His new shed and greenhouse were magnificent, but they lacked the feeling of the old one. His old potting shed had been a part of him and could never be replaced. Linda had appeared briefly in the doorway looking like nothing on earth with her hair all over the place and wearing a short skirt that drew attention to her fat thighs. Linda shrieked as soon as she caught sight of herself.

"What *do* I look like?"

"A right mess," said Malcolm. "You'd better tidy yourself up a bit if you're going to work for that chap next door. He won't appreciate seeing the top of your legs"

"Well, *you* won't have anything to worry about, *will* you?"

Malcolm pulled a face. "And nor will any one else by the look of you."

Linda flounced off into the kitchen and began to crash the dirty plates about in the sink. Mr Wentworth had a dish washer and when he was at work she would take her washing up round next door and put it in there. No more washing up for her.

Millie sat on the settee with Lucy to watch the first programme but there was very little of interest as far as she was concerned. All the men were doing was the initial clearing of the site. Suddenly there was a flash back to the original meeting of the residents and there was Julian Goodwood discussing the type of gardens he and Beatrice Thorn had hoped that people would like.

"Look, Mum! It's you, sitting on a cushion, you're talking to that man." Lucy was excited.

"What are you talking about?"

Millie looked at the scene, feeling embarrassed. Julian's interest in her was only too obvious and she hoped Mike wouldn't read too much in it when he saw it. At least she looked very serious and not at all encouraging.

"We were discussing your secret garden. They hadn't planned anything like that."

"And there's Mike and Mrs Fairweather. I think he's lovely, but she's horrible."

"You won't have her much longer, only a couple of weeks and she'll be gone."

"Will Mike go with her?"

"No, Lucy, he won't. He's coming to live with us, but you mustn't tell anyone at school. It's a secret until the holidays. Mrs Fairweather wouldn't like it if you told everybody would she."

Lucy was delighted. "Is he staying like the students?"

"No. I'm not taking the students any more after this term. He's coming to live with us for always I hope. He's going to look after us. We shall be his family and I hope we'll all be very happy together; do you understand?"

Lucy smiled. "Is that why you were kissing him the other day?"

Millie laughed. "I expect so. Something like that."

"He's much nicer than my real Dad. He'll never come back, will he?"

"No, never; Mike will take care of that. Oh, look! It's over and we missed the last bit. Now we'll have to wait until next week to see the next episode."

Venus was pleased with the first episode and hoped there would be some feed back from the papers, although it was early days yet. Comments in the newspapers could make or break a new programme. She had seen it happen so many times, when programmes had been shifted to less popular times.

Ed rang to get her opinion, and was pleased when she felt it had been a good start.

"Julian Goodwood has broken his contract with us," he told her. "Not that it matters. He was only going to make a few comments about the planting and string out a lot of incomprehensible names to terrify the viewers with his superior knowledge."

Venus laughed. "What reason did he give for not finishing his contract?"

"Oh, you'll like this! Apparently he went to the Bahamas on holiday and met a wealthy widow who asked him to plan her garden in Florida. It was too good a chance to miss."

"A widow; not his kind surely, although the money must have been tempting."

"And so was the widow, apparently. She's twenty four and worth a mint; a cool five million. She was on honeymoon with her ninety year old husband when he dropped down dead. Can you imagine it! He's going to marry her; trust Julian to get the best out of a deal."

"Killed him with kindness, did she?" laughed, Venus.

"An excess of something I reckon."

"Julian had better look out. She might be too much for him"

"Somehow I doubt that. He has a dreadful reputation where women are concerned."

"Where did you hear that?"

"Beatrice told me."

Venus roared with laughter. "Beatrice! However did *she* find that out? Nothing personal surely, as far as she was concerned."

"Apparently he chats up all the prettiest and sexiest ladies whenever they have worked together. Beatrice has had her work

Jan Pollard

cut out to keep him to heel. She respects his work but as a man she has no opinion of him."

"Well, she wouldn't would she. She's quite safe where he's concerned—oh, and now you're on the 'phone, Ed, could I mention our barbecue. Benji has suggested next Sunday afternoon. We've been having some good weather of late and it's supposed to be set fair for the rest of this week. I'll contact the neighbours if you think the film crew won't mind turning out on a Sunday. We'll feed them well."

"It'll mean paying them overtime but I think we can just about manage it. I'll leave it to you then. See you Sunday."

As predicted the sun shone on everyone on Sunday, and the barbecue was set up on the decking in the middle of Venus and Benji's garden. The flower beds were a blaze of colour. Everywhere there were clumps of red and orange poppies, and Canna lilies, with their paddle shaped leaves and red and orange flowers, standing in front of tree ferns and spotted laurel, vying for position with the spears of the red hot pokers.

Fiery red salvias took the eye amongst the less dominant flowers, while the long tassels of the love-lies-bleeding were beginning to show their tiny red flowers. Small red begonias and impatiens edged the sculptured beds of the garden, while fan palms, grown in pots, made an exotic background to the borders.

Over the fence trailed the climbing Spanish Flag plant, with its red and white and orange banana shaped blooms, and in its shade grew scarlet bergamot, teasing the senses with its aromatic foliage. Orange, red and yellow Mexican sunflowers grew in clumps amongst the smaller flowers and brightly coloured nasturtiums trailed around Scrumpi's play area, making it into an integral part of the garden.

By the embankment, at the end of the garden, a golden acacia tree stood proudly, its yellow leaves falling like a fountain of gold, and beside it a rowan tree had been planted, to make a show with its red berries in the autumn.

The mahogany coloured decking for the barbecue completed the effect of warmth, making the whole garden look as if it had been transported from the Caribbean.

The Hidden Gardens

Benji stood on the raised decking beside the enormous barbecue, resplendent in his white chef's hat and apron, turning the food as it cooked. The smell of spices wafted through the air, making everyone long to taste his offerings. This was going to be a barbecue to remember.

As they arrived the residents wandered amongst the flower beds or sat on the canvas chairs under tropical umbrellas to eat crispy home made potato chips, Caribbean grilled chicken, kebabs, Johnny cakes and coconut candy—all a speciality of West Indian cooking. There was a huge bowl of planter's punch made of ginger, rum, sugar and juices, to welcome everyone on their arrival, or if they preferred it there was Benji's home made ginger beer.

Everyone came except for Malcolm who objected to foreign food, and Edna, who knew nothing about it. They admired the garden, enjoyed the food and were fascinated by Scrumpi, who was wearing a dress to match her mothers', covered in a pattern of bright red poppies. On her head she wore red ribbons, tied onto her little bunches of hair, and as she staggered about on her baby legs and tumbled over, everyone found themselves picking her up from time to time, and found her quite enchanting.

Linda had come with Damian as Malcolm was being so unsociable. Millie brought Lucy, with instructions about keeping their distance from Mike, as Ruth and Beatrice would probably be there. As it happened, Ruth and Beatrice soon left, after Beatrice had taken Ruth round the garden to explain how it had been planned, and then Millie and Lucy were free to join up with him.

Malcolm could smell the delicious aroma of grilled spicy chicken wafting over his garden and began to feel hungry. To his annoyance Linda had left him nothing to eat, and he decided to change his mind and go round to the barbecue. At least he could see their garden and get some idea of the opposition, even if he refused their foreign food. To Linda's enormous surprise she saw him arrive and accept a glass of punch from Venus. The rumbling in his stomach had got the better of him and he took one of Benji's pieces of spicy chicken, which turned out to be

Jan Pollard

much better than he had ever imagined. Malcolm ate a second piece and then a third and remarked to Linda that it might be a good idea if they bought a barbecue for themselves.

"You could use it on your patio, Linda. We could eat outside like this sometimes ourselves. What do you think?"

Linda didn't know what to think. He had made all that fuss about having a patio for her flowers and now he was suggesting they bought a barbecue to use on it. She never knew where she was with Malcolm.

"It's gone six," said Venus. "The park will be closed by now, so I'm going round to see if I can find Edna. She's the only one of us who hasn't come round, apart from Mr De Courcy and he is on holiday so I understand. Please enjoy yourselves while I try to find her."

Linda looked sadly at Damian. It must be so difficult for him to have to tell such lies to excuse his past friend's absence. She noticed that Mr Fairweather was talking to him and feared correctly, that he was asking poor Mr Wentworth where his friend had gone to on holiday simply to make conversation. Damian bore up nobly. Linda gave him an encouraging smile which Damian chose to ignore as he moved away to refill his glass and drown his sorrows.

Venus picked up Scrumpi and walked round to the garden of Number 12, to find Edna sitting on her garden seat watching the fountain splashing gently into the small pool in the centre of the healing garden. She sat Scrumpi down on the seat between them and hoped her presence would remind Edna of their meeting in the park.

"Would you like to come round to our house, Edna? We're having a party; just the people who live along here in the terrace. We can't leave you out, can we?"

Edna seemed unwilling to get up. She was perfectly content sitting in her garden which had been made by the boy next door without her having anything to do with it. Venus decided to leave her where she was; seeing so many people together in one place might be too much for her.

The Hidden Gardens

"You know where I live, don't you, Edna? I'm just three doors along from you. You can always come and see me, and Scrumpi, if you want to. Don't forget."

Taking hold of Scrumpi's hand Venus walked back along the embankment. Edna watched them go. There was something about Venus that reminded her of a big coloured nurse who had looked after her a long time ago when she had been shut up in that place. It was after the baby had died and she had become so ill that they had taken her away, but it was so long ago that Edna had forgotten her name. The nurse had been very kind to her then and Edna wondered if perhaps she had come back to look after her again although it had been such a long time ago her memory, like most things, was lost in the mists of time.

CHAPTER 14

Alice Collins switched on the television in her flat, to watch the newest instalment of 'Looking at Your Backyard'. It was strange how differently she felt now she had left home in such a hurry; so anxious to leave to live with her lover, Mr Euan Jones, who had been her science master at the comprehensive. It had been odd looking at the people she had known as their neighbours talking about their gardens and what they hoped they would turn out to look like eventually. It was even more peculiar to watch her mother on the screen, getting all enthusiastic about having a patio and planting out her pots with that large lady telling her just what to do, as if she was a child. It made Alice feel as if she was back home again and a little less home sick. She had never realised how much she would miss her mother by running away like that.

 The baby began to grizzle in his carrycot and she picked him up to comfort him. He suffered from colic and was a very discontented baby. Although she loved him, Alice wished she had never become pregnant. Mr Jones, as she still thought of him, left her on her own most of the time. He had been very angry when she had told him that she was pregnant and as her stomach grew larger and larger and he found making love to her a joyless experience, he desisted altogether. Euan Jones liked young,

The Hidden Gardens

slim, over sexed teenagers, and there were plenty of them only too anxious to throw themselves into his arms at his new school. Alice and his unwanted baby were surplus to requirements. He already had an ex-wife and three children to support and now there was this new child who was always crying. The baby was born five weeks earlier than anticipated; a little shrimp of a thing, with none of his good looks that he could discern at present. Alice had just brought the baby home from hospital and he had been appalled by her lack of expertise. She was definitely not a born mother and needed her own mother to help her to look after this child. He decided that Alice should return home and told her as much, in the deep Welsh voice which had once thrilled her to the core and which nowadays only kept telling her what she was to do, as if he was her father. In fact he grew more like her father every day; a right grumpy, bossy old man. Alice wondered what she had ever seen in him during the heady days when he had made love to her in the locked science laboratory after the school day was over. He had told her that he loved her then, but since he had heard about the baby he had never mentioned that word again.

Looking at the opening shot as the programme started Alice began to come to her senses. That's where *she* should be right now; not here in Cardiff, where she knew nobody and they spoke in a way which made her feel like a stranger.

William was talking about the herbs in the healing garden he had planted, and he seemed to know an awful lot about them. Alice watched, fascinated by his self confidence. He had never been like that when she had lived at home. He was terrified of their dad and would never say boo to a goose. She used to answer their dad back but William knew better than that and never spoke unless necessary. This William on the telly was someone she had never seen before so perhaps things were better at home since she had left. Most of the rows had been about her having an affair with Mr Jones. It would be different now. The affair was over for both of them, not only for him, and it was time she left. When he came home tonight from what he had told her was a staff meeting, she intended to sort things out with him. He would have to pay for her to go back home with the baby and pay her an allowance for his child as well, so they could live. She dreaded her dad's wrath when she appeared with a new baby, but her mum would be pleased. Her mum loved babies, but she might not like becoming a grandmother all of a sudden. Alice decided that was a risk she would have to take. She would take her screaming bundle of joy home and her mum would have to look after him. The baby was already beginning to get her down and nothing she did for him stopped him crying.

Linda was just beginning to walk up the garden with Mr Wentworth's after dinner tray of tea, when she heard a terrible din coming from over the fence. Malcolm was shouting and swearing at someone in what Linda recognised as one of his uncontrolled outbursts of temper, and she hoped he wasn't having a go at William. It was too bad, just as Mr Wentworth had sat down in his gazebo for a bit of peace and quiet.

She put down the tray on the white wrought iron table and apologised for her husband. She wanted to keep this job and not lose it because of Malcolm.

"I'm so sorry, Mr Wentworth. Something terrible must have happened for Malcolm to carry on like that. He'll calm down eventually; he always does."

"Do you think you should perhaps just pop round and see what's happening, Linda. I'm not used to hearing such language and the sooner he stops swearing the better or I shall have to go indoors."

"Of course, Mr Wentworth, thank you, Mr Wentworth, I won't be a minute."

Linda went round via the embankment which was far quicker than going all the way round the front, to find out what was the trouble, and was amazed to find it was Alice's arrival back home that had caused all the fuss. Linda rushed to embrace her daughter almost falling over the carrycot in her haste.

"A baby!" shrieked, Linda. "What's this baby doing here?"

"It's mine of course, Mum; who else's baby did you think it was?"

"And she can clear off with it right away. I've been telling her that, Linda. We aren't having her squalling brat in our house. She's not coming home just when she thinks she will with her kids. We don't want them here, or her, for that matter."

"Oh, Malcolm; have a heart. Where else can she go at this time of the day? She'll have to stay tonight at least until we can sort her out."

"I should have sorted her out a long time ago, and now it's too late. Just listen to the noise that kid is making. Do something, Linda."

Linda picked up the baby, put him over her shoulder and patted his back, and the wailing calmed down.

"Poor little mite. What's his name, Alice?"

"Dylan; it's a Welsh name. Mr Jones said Dylan Thomas had been one of their most famous poets, so he wanted him called, Dylan."

"Mr Jones! You mean to tell us that Mr Jones is his father!! That dirty old man! So for all your talk you *were* having an affair with him when you were underage. You can leave now, Alice. I never want to see your face again." Malcolm threw down his hoe and went in through the back door and out of the front, to go to the pub, where he would find all the sympathy he felt he deserved.

Linda suddenly remembered Mr Wentworth. She had said she would be back soon and she felt he should be given some kind of explanation as to what had happened.

"Come with me, Alice. I'm taking the baby round next door to show Mr Wentworth. He might know what we should do now your father has been so unhelpful. He's such a kind man, and so clever. He has a bookshop, you know."

"Isn't he one of those gay men who lived next door?"

"Now don't talk like that, Alice. He's all on his own. His friend left him and he got very upset and now I look after him. We get on very well together."

Alice was surprised. "Have you left Dad then, to live with a —."

"Oh, Alice, don't be stupid! I'm his housekeeper."

Jan Pollard

Alice stared at her mother. She did look different now she thought about it; much tidier than she used to be and there was an air of responsibility about her.

"What about the launderette, then? Did you give that up?"

"Oh, no, it gave me up; it closed."

By this time they had reached the back of Damian's garden. Alice stood and stared. It was so beautiful with the water splashing over the fountain and into the channels. The programme about the garden fountains had still to be shown on the television and this was all new to her.

"Isn't it lovely," said Alice, admiringly.

Damian looked round. Linda had returned with a baby over her shoulder which appeared to have fallen asleep, and a young woman, whom he presumed to be her long lost daughter, Alice. So that was what the row had been all about. The prodigal had returned, but why they had come round to see him he could not imagine.

"Sorry to have left you for so long, Mr Wentworth. This is our Alice and her baby, Dylan, my grandson." Linda smiled, proudly. "We didn't know she was coming and Malcolm is being difficult. She has nowhere to stay. Her Dad won't have her in the house and she can't sleep on the street. It's too late to find her a hostel or somewhere like that. Can you suggest something?"

Damian was put out. How should he know where to put a homeless girl and her bastard son so late in the day? To-morrow he would make some enquiries and give Linda the day off to take her daughter to the Social Services or maybe the police would know of places where they would take her in. The baby woke up and began to grizzle again. Linda put her finger in his mouth and he sucked on it as if he was starving.

"Are you feeding him, Alice?"

"Yeah, but he's never satisfied. I haven't got enough for him. I need boobs like yours, mum. Mine need filling out."

Linda gave a sharp, dry cough. "Can we use your kitchen, Mr Wentworth? I'm sorry to ask but I don't expect you'd want her to feed the baby out here and I don't want to go back next door in case Malcolm comes home."

The Hidden Gardens

"Certainly, go ahead." The last thing Damian wanted to see was this girl feeding her baby at the breast. When they had gone he sat for a while and thought about it. He had two empty bedrooms, and as long as it was only for one night, he would let the girl stay as long as Linda stayed too, to keep an eye on her.

Linda came out to clear away his tray and fussed around. It was obvious she had no idea what to do about the situation. Damian decided he would have to do something about it himself and made the suggestion that they both stayed for one night only. Linda was overjoyed and rushed into the kitchen to tell Alice who had felt all along that something would turn up.

"I'll make up the beds, Alice, and put you in the big room with the baby. He'll have to sleep in the carrycot. I'll be in the little room if you need me but you must try not to let the baby cry too much if you can help it. Mr Wentworth knows nothing about babies. To-morrow we'll see what we can do about getting him onto a bottle and see the clinic about his care. You need something for his colic. It doesn't last for ever but it's not very nice for the poor baby while he suffers from it."

Alice went to bed feeling as if everything was going to turn out right now she was back with her mother. She hoped she might get a flat so her mother could come and baby sit in the evenings and she could get back to a normal life, living it up at the clubs with her old friends. Before long she'd find another boy friend, but next time she wouldn't get caught out and fall for a baby. This one was quite enough.

The baby had a restless night, which was usual, and Linda was up nursing him and comforting him while Alice slept. She hoped that Mr Wentworth had slept well too. He deserved to after his kindness.

In the early hours the baby fell into a deep sleep and Linda dozed off, briefly. At seven, she dressed and took a cup of tea to Damian who was still in bed, and asked him to give her his order for breakfast. As she was in the house she might as well provide him with his breakfast before he rushed off to Westminster. Damian was touched by her thoughtful manner. Guy had used to bring him an early cup of tea in the mornings. It was some time now since he had enjoyed such a luxury and he had missed it. Usually he grabbed a cup of coffee and a piece of toast before he went, leaving Linda to clear away when she came in to begin work. Today Linda was cooking him eggs and bacon; what a treat!

"I've told Alice not to use the bathroom until you have finished, Mr Wentworth, and she will stay upstairs until you have gone so as not to trouble you. I will find her somewhere else to stay today, but I hope to be back in time to get you your evening meal before I leave."

"Thank you Linda. If ever you would like to extend your working hours to staying overnight that would be fine by me. You could have Guy's larger room where you would be more comfortable. I would then pay you as a live-in housekeeper which would suit me well."

"I would like that very much, Mr Wentworth. William will soon be off my hands, and as soon as I can arrange it with Malcolm I will come."

Linda popped back home to sort Malcolm out before he left for work. Malcolm was still asleep in his chair downstairs, having come home too drunk the previous night to ascend the stairs, so her absence had not been noticed. She made him some sandwiches for his lunch in case he decided to go to work later and returned next door to make her lazy daughter get out of bed. She changed the baby, gave him to Alice to feed, and then set off with Alice and her new grandson to find a place for them both to live. They were not coming back to Mr Wentworth's house if she could help it. Linda had decided that she was going to live there herself in future, away from her belligerent husband and her troublesome daughter, and they could get used to it. It was lovely to find she had a grandson, and lovely to have Alice home again, and she would see them as much as possible but she would keep them at arm's length. It was time she had a life of her own without being bullied and pushed around any more and she had Mr Wentworth to thank for that.

Linda and Alice found someone to give them some help at the Social Services and Alice was taken to a women's hostel for young mothers, which caused Alice to turn up her nose as soon as it was suggested. However, she soon settled down when she found one of her friends there in the same predicament.

"Fancy seeing you here, Lynn," exclaimed Alice, watching her old friend changing her baby girl. "I didn't know you'd fallen for a baby."

"I knew you had," said her friend. "You told me before you left to go to Cardiff. Don't you remember? I suppose our Mr Jones sent you packing."

"In a way; it wasn't the same after the baby was born."

"I didn't think it would be. He didn't even suggest that I went to Cardiff with him when I told him I was pregnant."

Alice looked up in horror. "You mean he was having it off with you too?"

"Randy old goat; wasn't he just!"

The two girls fell into each other's arms, laughing with surprise at such a discovery.

"So our two kids are related then! Would you believe it!" and they began to laugh all over again as if it was the greatest joke in the world.

CHAPTER 15

Benji strapped Scrumpi into her pushchair and wheeled her slowly down the garden. The sunshine in June had made her sleepy and Venus liked her to have as much fresh air as possible. Today, Benji was in charge of his daughter for most of the day while the editing of the programme was going on in the studio. The last few programmes still had to be shown to the public but the project was coming to an end. There were only two more programmes to be filmed; the penultimate one where the public were invited to come and see all the gardens for themselves if they wished to, before voting for the winner, and the grand finale where the winner was announced and a well known television personality would present them with the cup and a framed certificate, to which only the residents and the makers of the programme would be invited.

Benji wanted to get on with his cooking. The marinade would be ready by now and it was time to add the shrimps and then grill them, after which he had to write out the recipe before he forgot all the details. Scrumpi was an angelic child and no trouble to either of her parents but there were times when Benji needed to be on his own, and this was one of them.

He parked Scrumpi under the shade of the golden acacia at the end of the garden. She was fast asleep and he decided to leave her there for half an hour before he returned to look at her. He could see her through the French windows which were wide open to let in the afternoon breeze, and he would hear her when she woke up. Even the city trains as they clattered along the line never woke her up as she took her afternoon sleep. Benji gave her a last loving look, and returned to his cooking. He would have at least half an hour of uninterrupted peace if all went well.

Edna decided to return home early. It was so hot in the park and there were some noisy children playing on skate boards tearing up and down the paths. She decided it would be much nicer to sit in her own garden and contemplate the cooling water from her fountain as it splashed into the bowl beneath. Edna had no idea how it worked. She never had to turn anything on or off—it just came on all on its own and gave her a great deal of pleasure. When the water butt ran dry she could fill her kettle there. It would be very useful.

Edna sighed contentedly and fell asleep in the sunshine. When she awoke she decided to see if she could find that nice person who had been so kind to her the other day; the black lady with the dear little baby. She had told her to come and see her whenever she liked, and she lived just along the back somewhere. Edna had seen her going along the embankment with the baby. Edna loved the baby; she was so fat and cuddly with a lovely smile. She had once had a baby like that a long time ago.

Edna got up, picked up her bag and set off along the embankment. She passed gardens and stopped to look at them. One was full of vegetables and she decided to help herself to a few lettuces while she was there. Nobody was around and she presumed they were for anyone to take. Whoever would want all those lettuces! There were enough to feed hundreds of rabbits!

The next garden had nothing in it to eat at all, so Edna passed it by. Then she came to a garden full of the most beautiful flowers and there was the baby. Edna was enchanted. The baby was strapped in her pushchair, wide awake, waving her chubby little arms at her as if she wanted to be picked up. She was all alone at the top of the garden which was strange. Edna had no idea where her mother could be so there was nobody to ask if she could take her for a walk and she decided to take her into the park to feed the ducks. The baby had liked feeding the ducks she seemed to remember.

With some difficulty she managed to release the brakes and set off along the embankment until she came to the little passage way beside her house. It was much easier getting the pushchair along there. She crossed the road and went through the park gates and pushed Scrumpi towards the pond where she sat down on her usual seat and began to feed the ducks. Scrumpi chortled with pleasure and tried to touch the ducks as they waddled round her. Edna gave her some bread to throw to them which sometimes ended up in Scrumpi's mouth and sometimes landed on the path where it was quickly gobbled up. Both Edna and the baby were having the greatest fun. Nobody took much notice of them as from a distance Edna looked like the child's grandmother, with her discoloured skin, due to years without proper washing, and her white hair.

Benji finished what he was doing and looked up the garden. Scrumpi had made no noise so he had presumed she was still asleep. He had looked only a few minutes ago and she had been there, lying under the shade of the golden acacia tree, but now she had definitely gone. Benji panicked and ran along the embankment in both directions. Scrumpi was nowhere to be seen. He looked down onto the rail track, terrified that she might have moved her pushchair to the edge by wriggling her legs to move it along and thanked all the powers that be that she was not there. He looked in all the gardens in case Venus might have returned and taken her with her, but he knew Venus would have told him first.

Benji picked up the telephone and rang the studio. He was in such a state he could scarcely speak when Venus answered. Venus told him to ring the police while she got back as soon as she could. Ed brought her home and tried to calm them both until the police arrived. It was obvious that their baby had been abducted and Benji wept, feeling as if he had been to blame. The open embankment was a temptation to anyone to walk along the backs of the houses although hardly anyone ever came there as the fences, when they were in place, made it almost impossible to walk on the narrow piece of ground without the danger of falling onto the line below.

As soon as the police arrived they searched all the gardens and knocked on all the doors to speak to those residents who were in and everyone joined in the search but there was no sign of Scrumpi. As the hours passed Venus and Benji became more and more frantic until Venus suddenly remembered Edna and her seat in the park. She and Benji ran through the gates and there was Edna sitting on her usual seat with Scrumpi in her pushchair. Their initial relief turned into panic when they realised that Scrumpi had wriggled herself in her pushchair until it was on the very edge of the pond, as she had tried to touch the waddling ducks.

Benji ran as fast as he could and caught her just before the pushchair tumbled into the water. Scrumpi laughed and chortled to see her father, totally unaware that she had been in any danger.

"How dare you take her away, Edna!" screamed Venus. "She's not *your* baby. You nearly drowned her."

Edna got up and began to shuffle away. The person she had liked so much and whom she had thought was a nurse was angry with her. She hadn't done anything wrong had she? The baby had loved the ducks and they had enjoyed the afternoon together. The baby was laughing so why was everyone so angry with her? Edna felt very unhappy. Then a police woman took hold of her arm and tried to put her in a car. Edna cried out with fear. She wanted to go home. Where were they going to take her? Back to that place again where she had lived all those years ago?

Venus saw her distress and spoke to the police. "There's something wrong with Edna. I don't know what it is but she needs help. Scrumpi's safe and sound with her father so I'll go to the police station with Edna. She can't go alone; just look at her, poor thing."

Edna was crying quietly, her tears streaking her not too clean face.

"I know I was cross with her but I'm sure she meant no harm to Scrumpi. She loves her in her own way. She just needs someone to help her. We all think that along the terrace but nobody knows what to do about it."

"If you're sure you want to come; abduction is a crime, you know. She should be charged."

"Oh, no, not poor Edna; we wouldn't want that. Let's talk about it when we get to the station."

Edna looked terrified as they were shown into an interview room and Venus held her hand to comfort her. Nobody knew anything about her, Venus explained, and most people thought she was a squatter who lived in squalor in the end house.

A policewoman looked inside Edna's copious straw bag and gasped at what she could see inside. Amongst the slices of bread were hundreds of notes and coins, and two pension books in the names of Edna Schwartz and Franz Schwartz of Number 12 Park Close, North Acton.

"Is that your name?" she asked Edna. Edna nodded.

"And is Franz Schwartz your husband?" Edna nodded again.

"She lives on her own. I'm sure of that," said Venus. "We've never seen anyone else come out or go into the house, but I saw her drawing two pensions at the post office the other day."

"Where is your husband?" asked the policewoman.

Edna shook her head. "I dunno: he not come home for a long time now."

"Look, we'll put her in a safe hostel, give her a bath and find her something clean to wear while we have a search of her property. You'd be surprised what we find sometimes, and it's not always very palatable. We'll try and find her husband, if he isn't dead. If he is she shouldn't be drawing his pension. She could be in deep trouble if that's what she's been up to."

"Can I come with her to the hostel? She knows me, I'm a neighbour, and I think she trusts me. I'm sure she hasn't meant to do anything wrong, she just doesn't understand many things. Her memory seems to have gone."

"Not gone enough to defraud the Inland Revenue it would seem."

Venus gave up. How could she defend Edna? She knew nothing about her. She would accompany her to wherever she was being taken and leave her there to be looked after and then keep in touch and hope that her life would be sorted out. It was time that someone took care of Edna, now she was unable to care for herself.

The news about Edna spread along the terrace like wildfire. The house at Number 12 belonged to her and her husband, but nobody could remember seeing him apart from Millie, who wondered if the reclusive people who had once lived there during her childhood had been Edna and her husband. It was a possibility as those people had a foreign sounding name, which she had long since forgotten.

Venus was worried as they had taken it upon themselves to clear Edna's garden and plant it without her permission. They had even thrown her old pram into the skip thinking it was rubbish which had been dumped there.

Ed told her to ask Edna if she had minded when she went to see her. He doubted that she would make a complaint. She enjoyed sitting in her new garden on her new seat it would seem, so he felt sure all would be well. She thought that William from next door had made it for her out of kindness, so it was best she should continue to think that; at least it got them off the hook.

Venus went to visit her the next day only to find that Edna had been moved into a home for the elderly. After discovering her whereabouts she found Edna so confused by events that it seemed unkind to bring up the subject of the garden so it was never mentioned.

"I suppose her house will be sold now," she said to Benji. "The work on the garden should make it more saleable, so that makes me feel a bit better about it."

"When the garden is seen on the television buyers will be more interested in her poor old place so you'll have done her a favour; think about it like that. You've nothing to feel guilty about, my love."

Venus felt a bit better; her Benji could always see the best side of a situation.

When the police arranged to clear out Edna's house they found nothing of any consequence apart from piles of unopened

Jan Pollard

mail from many years ago and letters, yellow with age. From these letters they discovered that Edna had been released from the old mental institution into her husband's care, when the buildings were no longer used for patients, who had been placed into community care homes. There was nothing to tell them what had happened to her husband apart from a letter accepting his resignation from a firm of jewellers in the city. The jewellers were still in existence, and although Franz Schwartz had resigned twenty years previously, somebody might remember something about him.

Enquires were made and the previous owner who was now very old himself, was tracked down.

'I can remember Franz Schwartz,' he wrote, in reply to the police enquiry. *'He and his wife were interned with me at the onset of the last war, at a place called Port Erin on the Isle of Man, where we lived in a large run down hotel near the beach. Franz was a German Jew like myself, who fearing for his life had left Germany before war was declared, with his young wife, Edna. She was very young and cried so much, worried for her family whom they had left behind and whom they never heard of again. Like my own family they must have been taken to the concentration camps'*

At this point in the letter the writing became almost unreadable, as if the writer's hand trembled with the emotion of writing about such terrible experiences.

'When the war ended I started up my old business again and gave my friend Franz a position there. After the war many people needed money and sold me their old family jewellery which we broke up and made into smaller pieces. Franz was a clever designer and we began to make money and moved the firm into the city. Franz and Edna took a modest property in North Acton and all went well until Edna gave birth to a son and suffered from post natal depression. The baby died of a fever and she blamed herself and tried to commit suicide. Franz feared to leave her and she was locked away for her own safety.

The Hidden Gardens

Franz took her back home after the mental institution was closed and asked my son, who owned the business in those days if he could leave to care for his wife. That had been about fifteen years ago. Since then I have heard nothing of them. I have written but I have never received any replies so I presumed they must have moved or were no longer alive.'

The police filed the letter. Franz Schwartz would be presumed dead unless any further information came their way, which was extremely doubtful considering his age.

Edna was given a social worker to see to her needs after her history was discovered. The front door of Number 12 was made safe and the broken windows were boarded up. Edna would never come home again. Her furniture, or what remained of it was taken away and the house was put up for sale, to help to pay for her keep.

Venus met the social worker on her next visit to Edna.

"Have you any idea what happened to her husband?"

"He's been listed as a missing person; that's all I can tell you. The police have no idea why he left her. Nobody seems to know what happened to him. Why he left her alone is a mystery; your guess is as good as mine. Perhaps he had been killed in an accident and had nothing on his person to identify him, or looking after Edna had become too much for him. She will only say that he never came home one day."

"Poor Edna; left alone for years to manage on her own."

The social worker nodded and sketched out Edna's past history so Venus would have some idea as to why no owner of Number 12 could be found despite the search by the television company.

"And yet the owner was there all the time," mused Venus. "Nobody thought it could be Edna. Not in their wildest dreams."

"Amazing isn't it. The water and electricity had been cut off years ago when the bills ceased to be paid. The council considered the property to be derelict and had decided the owners had moved away and just left it in that state. We can't think how she managed. There was an old oil stove and plenty of candles and matches but no heating; she'll be fine now, once she's settled down. It's good to know she has one friend who cares about her."

Venus smiled. "Her immediate neighbour, Mrs Collins, kept an eye on her too, not that there was much she could do. Edna wasn't exactly co-operative."

It was strange how this development affected the other residents of Park Close. Most of them had wanted their 'squatter' to leave because she lowered the tone the area but once they heard her sad history from Venus they felt differently. Perhaps they should have alerted the authorities once they had realised her sad circumstances but nobody had wanted to be the one to take it up with the Social Services. It had seemed like interfering and they had their own lives to lead anyway.

"No wonder she never wanted to speak to people," said Venus. "Perhaps she was afraid we would tell the SS about her and she would be taken away to a concentration camp. Poor Edna; who could tell what went on in her head."

"I really tried to be kind to her," said Linda, when she heard the story. "I used to take her things to eat but she never thanked me; she was like that."

"I'm sure you were," said Damian. "You're the kindest person I've ever known. What would *I* do without you?"

Linda had smiled. Damian would never have to be without her; she would see to that. Looking after him was the best job in the world and she had never been so comfortable in all her life. He had even taken her out in his posh car on Sundays to visit grand gardens and houses, the like of which she had never imagined existed.

Malcolm had a pretty good idea as to who had trampled all over his lettuces when he came home to see that some of them had been ripped out of the ground. At first he had thought it was done out of spite by one of the other garden owners who didn't want him to win the cup, but once he had heard how Edna had taken that Nigerian woman's baby away he realised it must have been her.

"I thought it had been Edna," he told Linda, after accusing everyone else. "She's crazy. It's a good job she's been taken away."

"It might be a good job someone's going to look after her now, Malcolm, but she never did anyone any harm and it's a pity you didn't show her a bit more kindness."

"Didn't do anyone any harm! She took that Nigerian woman's baby away, didn't she? That's what you told me."

"She's Jamaican, Malcolm. I keep telling you that, but you don't listen."

"What's the difference?"

"Quite a lot I should think if you're Jamaican. Anyway she didn't mean to hurt the little girl, she just took her for a walk."

"Well I'm glad she did as it happens because we might have some new neighbours who won't keep their back yard like a tip."

"You don't know that. It might be let to a load of students now Millie Carrington's not going to take in any more of them."

"How do you know that?"

"She told me. She's got other plans apparently, although she didn't say what."

Ruth was pleased to see the back of Edna, and was glad to hear the Social Services were at last doing their job as far as Edna was concerned. They should have been aware of her years ago and taken her away from Park Close.

"She lowered the tone of the place," she told Beatrice. "I kept telling Mike we should do something about her but he had no interest in getting in touch with anyone and if I'd done something myself he would never have backed me up. He preferred to turn a blind eye; he always took the easiest way out of everything."

"Sounds just like a man; you're better off without him, my dear."

"Thank goodness the house sale is sorted out at last. In two weeks time we shall be in Kyoto and can leave all this behind. I've told him that I don't expect anything of his to be left here when we get back. I want him gone: like Edna!"

"Dearest, Ruth, if it hadn't been for the programme we would never have met. It's simply amazing what flowers can do; it's brought us together, and what could be more wonderful than that."

Jan Pollard

"Nothing," said Ruth, as she kissed her, "just, nothing."

Millie had been glad to hear from Venus about Edna's new home and hoped she would be happy there, but there was something else troubling Venus when she had come to see her. The Dutch police had been in touch with the television company after Lucy's father had been seen on the television, taking part in a gardening programme which involved Millie and her daughter. Ed sent Venus to tell Millie about their call.

"We don't know what it's all about, Millie, but it's something really serious. The police asked us to give them details of you and Lucy as he might still be around, especially as Lucy told Ed he was her father. It's none of our business but we felt you should be told as they want to contact you."

"Oh, my God! I knew there was something wrong when he arrived. He told me some tale about his wife leaving him and taking their son away and he asked to come and see Lucy, as Lucy is his child, although he left me before she was born. I could see it had nothing to do with him seeing Lucy when he arrived. He was running scared. He was running away from something. I was frightened of him, with good reason. Mike, bless him, booted him out. I don't know where he is now."

"He certainly acted in a strange way when we were filming; didn't want to be seen I suppose."

"Obviously not," Millie felt a chill of fear creep over her just thinking about it.

"Well, thank you Venus, for telling me. I shall expect a visit from them in due course, I would imagine."

Venus left, somewhat surprised to hear that Mike Fairweather had been the reason for Millie's unwanted guest leaving her house. She was aware of his wife's friendship with Beatrice Thorn, but rarely saw Ruth to read anything more into it. Now she wondered, as it would appear that Millie and Mike were getting together. Her idea for the programme seemed to have done a great deal more than sorting out people's backyards; it had sorted out the people themselves and all for the better, she hoped.

The Hidden Gardens

Millie was unable to help the Dutch police in their search for Ian Francis. The last she had seen of him had been his back disappearing down her staircase, and she never wanted to see him again. When she was told how his wife's remains had been discovered in a dyke she was horrified to think she had given him sanctuary, and even allowed him to take Lucy out on his own. It made her shudder to think what might have happened to them both and she was determined never to tell Lucy.

She had asked about his son. What had happened to his little boy? Surely he hadn't murdered him too? Then she was told he had no children and nor had his wife. It had all been a fantasy dreamed up to make her feel sorry for him. Millie was furious with herself for having been taken in so easily.

The police assured her it would only be a matter of time before they caught up with him. It was a pity the insurance company had not informed them sooner once they became suspicious of the claim on his wife's policy. She was to alert the English police should she hear from him again as they were in touch with them about the case.

Millie was thankful Mike would be with her very soon now. What ever would have happened to her if he hadn't been there? Just thinking about it was frightening enough.

CHAPTER 16

Ed had decided to open the gardens on the second Sunday in June for the public to come and view them if they wished before telephoning in their votes, and he hoped they would have good weather. The photographers would be there early to take shots of the owners of each garden for the book which was soon to be published, as well as the film crew, who would stay longer to film the public arriving and hear some of their comments for the penultimate programme.

Beatrice was delighted at the choice of date as her precious Japanese irises should be in bloom around the pool; the Caprician Butterfly and the Sea Empress, with their petals like silk handkerchiefs, and the Great Mogul with its beautiful purple colouring and the blue Landscape at Dawn. Even their names evoked the mysteries of the East.

She had bought a kimono for Ruth to wear for the occasion; red silk embroidered with birds of paradise, with a gold obi of embroidered brocade, and she had arranged for a Japanese woman to come and dress her hair, who knew how a geisha would have it arranged. Ruth would hold a samisen as if she was playing it, and hide her face behind a fan if the visitors to the teahouse asked too many questions. A hidden tape would play the plink plonk sounds of the samisen as she mimed the movements.

The Hidden Gardens

Ruth, who had been interested in teaching drama, was thrilled with the idea. Beatrice was not dressing up. She felt as if a kimono would not suit her large figure, and she doubted that she could get an obi to fit around her waist whereas Ruth, with her slender figure and her small feet would look perfect in the part. Instead Beatrice intended to take people round her Japanese garden and to tell them about the plants and the ideas behind its construction. Winning the cup would be an acknowledgement of her merit as a landscape gardener and would help her to be sought after for future contracts, if all went well.

It was a pity that the bamboo fence along the back would not be in place to finish off the look of the garden but it was only possible for the public to enter the gardens from the embankment side. Ed had promised Venus that the fences would be replaced the next day so there would never be another opportunity for anyone to take Scrumpi away again. All the residents were glad to hear that their privacy would soon be ensured as well as the safety of their property. That had been the only problem with the makeover and one which had not become too apparent until Scrumpi had disappeared. The public who were coming to wander round their gardens were an unknown quantity, and people had been known to steal cuttings and even plants on such occasions.

Just before the opening Millie decided there was something missing in her garden. She had walked along the embankment one evening to look at the other gardens and seen the bamboo waterfall and the Persian fountain and even Edna's little solar fountain working away although there was nobody left to enjoy it. It was a pity she had no water feature in her garden and she wished she had thought about it before.

Unfortunately she had spent her garden allowance so she would have to organise something herself. She spoke to Mike about it and they took Lucy to a local garden centre to see what they could find that would be simple for Mike to fix. Here they found a little DIY fountain that bubbled out of a pile of shiny stones. Mike bought it for Lucy and without too much trouble fixed it up in her secret garden. Lucy and Mike worked together

Jan Pollard

piling up the stones around the tiny nozzle, and were thrilled when the water began to bubble out of it. Millie, watching them find so much pleasure in each other's company knew that Lucy had accepted him. Happiness for all of them was just around the corner.

Cars blocked Park Close and along all three sides of the park, where parking was permitted, and filled all the car parks in the area on the day the gardens were opened. People poured in from the buses and the trains and coaches, which had been booked for the occasion. The police were on duty everywhere and the public were only allowed to stay in each garden for a matter of minutes, as there were so many. They were directed into Millie's garden and trailed through the gardens in turn, coming out along the passageway beside Edna's garden. Some visitors expected cream teas to be served but there was no room for such delights and they were directed to the tea shop in the parade which did a roaring trade that afternoon and set out tables and chairs and umbrellas along the entire length of the pavement in continental fashion.

Benji was very popular. He was well known from his television series and many people had come especially to see him in the flesh. He was delighted to show them the herb garden he had made in front of his kitchen window, next to Scrumpi's play area. Beatrice had suggested the herbs and the lay out, and he found it invaluable. He was happy to point out the different kinds of herbs and their use to anyone who asked, and sold his recipe books from a large pile beside the back door, signing them for his fans.

"Why isn't there any water in this garden?" Venus was asked time after time by people who watched gardening programmes and expected that to be an essential part of a makeover.

"If you had a small child you'd know why," she replied. "I nearly lost my little girl in the pond in the park. Children love water but it's just not safe in a garden in my opinion. So there won't be any water here."

Some of the visitors had read about the incident in the paper and nodded understandably smiling at Scrumpi as she played,

The Hidden Gardens

close by her father, watching everyone pass by. Venus, who looked like a flower garden herself in her outfit, gave Scrumpi a swing from time to time in her play area, but never took her eyes off her for one moment.

Many of the visitors to the garden at Number 6 were West Indian, drawn by the bright colours of the flowers and the presence of Benji and Venus. One group introduced themselves as Benji's second cousin and his family, with whom he had lost touch since childhood and there was much laughter and back slapping, and a promise to keep in touch in future. This family had a beautiful long limbed daughter, named Connie, in whom Venus could see a family likeness to her own daughter. Connie seemed to love Scrumpi and made a great fuss of her and Venus could see the possibility of Connie maybe coming to look after her. The programme had taken off far better than Ed could have imagined and there would be more work for the studio in the future, which would mean she would need help with Scrumpi. It was quite extraordinary how her idea had flowered and things had come together.

Lucy had many visitors. It seemed as if all her class had come to see her willow arbour and to bask in her reflected glory. Lucy had never realised she had so many friends until now, as they sat in her secret garden and talked. It became a problem when people needed to walk into the next garden and Millie suggested they went along the passage to reach the Japanese garden next door once they had seen the secret garden through the archway. It seemed a shame to take away Lucy's obvious pleasure at becoming the centre of attraction.

Mike had come to share the afternoon with her as if it was perfectly natural for him to be there. They belonged together and felt in perfect harmony with one another as they walked amongst the sweet scents of the rose garden. He helped to explain about the roses to the visitors who showed an interest in the different types; their names, and the time of their flowering and their cultivation, as he had planted and cared for them himself.

As the visitors thinned out he sat with his arm around Millie under the pergola, feeling as if they had been together forever.

Ruth had no idea he was next door with Millie. As she and Beatrice prepared for the rush of visitors to their Japanese garden Mike's whereabouts were of no concern to her. In a few days time she would never have to see him again or even give him a thought. She had all she had ever wanted in life and that was Beatrice, and the exciting life they would spend together.

Getting dressed as a geisha was far more complicated than Ruth had ever imagined. The Japanese woman who was helping her to get prepared came early in the morning as the process took about half a day to complete. As her hair was long and black she was being made up to look like a maiko, with her hair piled up on the top of her head into an elaborate bun, smoothed over with camellia oil to give it a genuine sheen and then lacquered to keep each strand in place. To complete the effect a tortoiseshell comb decorated with pearls was tucked into the back and silk flowers would be put into place once she was dressed.

Her face was covered in a pink foundation over which thick white paste was applied, and a final dusting of white powder. Her eyes were outlined in black and rouge was dabbed beside each eye and beside her nose, and finally safflower petal lipstick was smoothed over her lips in a cherry red colour. Her dresser had brought some blackener for her teeth, which was traditional, but Ruth refused to wear it. She would never open her mouth if she was shown to have black teeth. A maiko might have black teeth but Ruth most definitely would not!

The beautiful silk kimono was wrapped round her, tucked in to fit and then tied into place. She slipped her feet into red thonged wooden clogs with four inch high heels, which showed that she was a first year maiko, or a trainee geisha, and tottered out of the room to show Beatrice the finished result. Beatrice was quite overcome for Ruth looked truly beautiful.

Ruth was helped across the stepping stones and was photographed on the little wooden bridge which spanned the stream, and then beside the teahouse, before she settled herself on the bamboo mat inside and took up her samisen in a typical pose. There were yet more photographs, and some with her hiding behind her fan.

Ed had been amazed at her transformation and called the film crew over, and Ruth had to repeat her performance all over again, only this time the music from the tape was playing as she pretended to pluck the strings of the samisen.

Hearing the sound of Japanese music from next door, Mike could hardly resist a look at what was going on and peered over the bamboo fence. Seeing Ruth posing by the teahouse he wondered who it was; probably an actress playing the part, and had no idea he was looking at the person who had once been his wife. Whoever it was she looked fantastic, and he decided they had no chance of the rose garden winning the cup.

He told Millie about it and she came to look over the fence, but Millie was unimpressed. There was only one person she was interested in winning, and that was the handsome, gorgeous man from next door. He had given her his heart and that was the same as winning the lottery as far as she was concerned.

Ruth settled herself down, ready to accept the amazed looks of the public as they crossed the little red painted bridge and came to the entrance of the teahouse, attracted by the sound of Japanese music. Seeing her there appeared to startle some people as they looked through the door and they hurried on to the next garden. Some were intrigued and stayed longer. Some asked questions to which Ruth gracefully bent her head, as if she had no knowledge of the language, and some took photographs. When there was a lull in the number of visitors coming through she took up her fan and fanned herself vigorously as the thick white make up made her feel very hot. She could only imagine that a real geisha made herself up like this for entertaining gentlemen in the evenings and certainly not on hot afternoons.

She became aware of footsteps coming across the gravel and picked up her samisen again to act the part.

"Ah, so," said a voice, as a Japanese gentleman entered the teahouse, clicked his heels together and bowed politely towards Ruth.

"A real live geisha; how delightful!"

Ruth nodded her head slightly in response to his compliment and continued to play her instrument, hoping he would soon leave. As it was getting close to the time when the gardens were closing there were no more visitors coming across the bridge and the Japanese gentleman took advantage of that fact and came to sit next to Ruth on the bamboo matting.

"You play like a professional," he said, admiringly. "I will pay you well to entertain my guests if you would agree."

From his wallet he took out a card and placed it in front of her. "You see, I am the owner of the best sushi restaurant in London."

Ruth, who was beginning to feel extremely uncomfortable, refused to look at the card, so it was waved in front of her face. She put down the samisen and hid behind her fan, forgetting that the tape was still playing, hidden under the folds of her kimono.

"Ah, so!" said her visitor, laughing. "You are a fake! You cannot play the samisen, but perhaps you can still entertain in other ways," and to Ruth's horror he began to pull at her obi. Ruth tried to get up but it was almost impossible to get to her feet in her high heeled wooden clogs. She kicked them off and struggled to get away but he was already trying to get his hands on the tape which he could see poking out of a fold in her kimono. She screamed for Beatrice and the sound stopped him for long enough for her to pick up the samisen and hit him on the side of his head. Hearing her shout for help and nursing his sore head her Japanese visitor decided to leave and made a hurried exit along the embankment. Beatrice, realising that something had gone horribly wrong tore after him but lost him as he darted through the park. On her return she found Ruth looking very bedraggled, sitting weeping with anger on the bridge. Her white face was streaked with black eye make up and the bun on top of her head had come awry. On her lap she held the broken samisen with its twisted strings, while the tape was still playing, adding insult to injury.

"My dear; oh, my poor dear," said Beatrice as she lifted her to her feet, "I would have stayed with you if for one moment I'd thought you were in any danger."

"He thought I was a real geisha," said Ruth, miserably, "and you know what men expect of them. He even left his calling card so I could contact him."

"If I'd have caught him I would have handed him over to the police." Beatrice was furious. "Come along, my dear; let me get you indoors."

"Can you find those uncomfortable shoes, Beatrice? I can't walk across the gravel without them. They're inside somewhere."

Beatrice picked up the shoes and the obi and then found the card. *'The Pearl of the Orient'* she read, *'Authentic Japanese food and entertainment.'*

She tore the card into shreds and went back to Ruth. Maybe he had been a genuine visitor to the gardens, knowing there would be a Japanese garden there for him to look around, but it was unfortunate that he had arrived at the end when most of the visitors had gone and spoilt what would have been a most successful afternoon. She had hoped to have the tea ceremony in the teahouse with Ruth that evening, when they would make their vows of everlasting love, but that would have to wait for another time. Ruth was far too upset by events to take part in anything, and needed tender loving care until she recovered.

Damian sat in lonely isolation in his gazebo at Number 8 Park Close, and listened to the water as it trickled over the sides of his Moorish fountain and ran along the blue channels between the well tended lawns. His garden was an earthly paradise and he wished he had Guy sitting there beside him on this special day to enjoy the beauty he had done so much to create, but it was no good thinking about Guy. He had been faithless and cruel and had been replaced by Linda. Dear kind Linda, who would never let him down. He had thought that once about Guy but he had been wrong. Linda was devoted to him in the nicest possible way. He found her physically repellent, being a woman who obviously had no dress sense and often annoyed him with her brainless chatter, but then he had no use for a woman in the physical sense and would never feel like that about any woman, now he had come to terms with his true self. As time went on he hoped that he might help Linda to choose her wardrobe and let him buy clothes for her, as a reward for her loyalty. He would prefer her to be addressed as his housekeeper if they went anywhere together, and not to be thought of as his wife, as had

Jan Pollard

happened on a few occasions lately, by strangers. Damian felt she could be educated to enjoy the better things in life if he took time to teach her. He frequently brought books home from the shop which he hoped she would look at, although she told him she was too busy these days with her own family and him as well, to look at books. Linda only looked at women's magazines or quickly flipped through a romance from Mills and Boon and was too considerate to ask him not to bother.

Damian had asked her to join him in the gazebo on this special day. He had put on a tape of music entitled, 'In a Persian Garden', to listen to as he drank his wine and did the Times crossword, but Linda had declined. She loved her tiny patio with its terracotta pots of flowers and her tropical umbrella. Sitting on her teak seat by her wooden fold up table with a cup of tea, she could chat to all and sundry and really enjoy herself. The visitors to Mr Wentworth's garden might want to talk to him about it and Linda felt she would be unable to cope. She would be better off next door with Malcolm's vegetables; not that she felt any interest in vegetables herself but she wanted to wear her Dolly Parton outfit for the occasion, which showed off her splendid cleavage and tiny waist. She felt that Mr Wentworth might be startled by the long blonde wig, which was a vital part of the outfit and refuse to recognise her which would be embarrassing for them both. Linda enjoyed dressing for the cameras and she intended to look her best on this occasion.

Malcolm was immensely proud of his garden now it was finished. He had spent every hour of daylight when he was home from work, getting it to perfection. His mates on the rail maintenance gang had missed all the fresh vegetables he used to sell to them in the past as these days his garden was kept in perfect order for the cameras to view. It was only when he thinned out his lettuces that he could spare them any, and they were poor specimens and only worth giving away. After the programme was over he would begin selling them again, but he hoped they would all come and support him on the 'Open Gardens' afternoon, and better still, ring in and vote for his garden.

The Hidden Gardens

Before the public were admitted Malcolm had a cup of tea with his wife, who was looking quite extraordinary in her wig.

"Have you dressed yourself up for that Mr Wentworth's benefit, Linda? You're nearly falling out of that top and the skirt is so short I don't know why you've bothered to put it on. Does he get you to dress up like a schoolgirl or a maid in a frilly pinafore to satisfy his secret longings?"

"I'm dressed like this for the camera, Malcolm. I like to think I can still look sexy, that's why. You never know but someone might take a fancy to me and offer me a part in a film, as a stand in. You used to like the way I looked. Mr Wentworth prefers me to dress modestly; he's most respectable, but I like to think that people notice me."

"There's no doubt about that, Linda; you'll be noticed all right this afternoon! I prefer to look at my courgettes and my marrows any day; at least they look natural."

Malcolm finished his cup of tea, thought he could see a weed and rushed to remove it. Linda cleared the tea things away, feeling peeved. It was obvious that Malcolm no longer loved her and she longed to be loved like most human beings but it looked as if she would have to make do with being a treasured member of Mr Wentworth's household for the rest of her life, which although being very pleasant indeed lacked the vital spark to set her pulses racing. She would never desert him; he had been so good to her, but somehow she would have to find a way to fill that part of her life which had been missing for such a long time, and that was being loved just for herself.

Malcolm's line maintenance gang all turned up to support him in the afternoon. They walked round his vegetables as Malcolm told them how he had grown them and the trouble he had taken over each and every one, as if they were his children. It was hot in the greenhouse but they were forced to stand and listen as Malcolm spoke at length about his tomatoes and his cucumbers. Some brought their wives who chatted to Linda while the important vegetables were discussed at length, and then Malcolm started on the soft fruit until there was a blockage in the line of people wanting to move on from the other gardens and Malcolm was forced to let them pass on their way.

There was a new member amongst Malcolm's work mates whom Linda had never seen before; a man of quite muscular proportions in his middle thirties, with a handsome face and a twinkle in his eye, who came over to introduce himself.

"Never knew old Malcolm had a wife who looked like Dolly Parton," he said, giving an admiring glance at her very obvious cleavage. "He's a lucky chap to come home to you."

"He doesn't," said Linda. "I work next door as Mr Wentworth's housekeeper, and I live there, but this is my patio and that's why I'm over here today."

"I see; and do you live *with* the gentleman in the Persian garden, if you don't mind me asking?"

"Goodness, no; I'm just his housekeeper: I told you." Linda gave him an encouraging smile. She liked the look of him; he was a large man and he had considerable sex appeal and what was even better, he had a way of making her feel special.

"I'll give a knock next door when I'm round this way, if I may, Dolly."

"I'm only dressed up like Dolly Parton for today," said Linda. "It's for the cameras you see, so I look a bit special; my name's Linda."

"You look very special to me, Linda. I'd like to get to know you a bit better. In fact there's a lot of you I'd like to get to know a bit better, if you know what I mean."

Linda laughed. He was very cheeky but he was her sort, all slap and tickle and happy to take her how she was; he was just what she had been wanting for a long time, a boyfriend with no responsibilities.

"Don't come on Sundays or Mondays because Mr Wentworth is home then, but during the week is fine, or Saturdays; he's at the shop all day then."

"I'll come next Saturday then and take you to Southend. How would you like that?"

Linda felt as if her heart would burst with happiness. Somebody actually wanted to be with her. Even if it didn't last long she would know what it meant to be loved again; to feel a man's arms around her, holding her close. When he had moved on with the crowd she suddenly realised she hadn't asked him his name. Malcolm would know but she wouldn't ask him. He probably wouldn't bother to answer if she did and what did it matter; he said he would come and Linda was sure he would keep his word.

William was feeling nervous and paced up and down the gravel paths as he waited for the crowd to descend upon the healing garden. He could hear his father talking to them at length all about his precious vegetables next door and it was only a matter of time before they came round the corner. William began to bite his nails with worry when, all of a sudden, the most beautiful dark skinned girl he had ever seen almost bounced into the garden, all on her own.

"Hi! You must be William," she said. "I've been watching you on the telly. I didn't bother with the other gardens. I just came to see you."

William swallowed hard. He had never had any success with girls up to now, being too shy to make an impression on any of them, and yet here was this goddess who had come simply to see him; or was it his healing garden she wanted to see. He wasn't too sure.

"I'm Connie, by the way. My real name is Convolvulus, but I'm always called Connie.

It's a twining plant you know. My Mum called me that because I had such long limbs when I was small and I used to wrap myself round people."

"Really!" said William, thinking that was highly unlikely until he looked at her shapely long legs. Well, she could wrap herself round him any time if she felt so disposed.

"Would you like me to give you a tour round the garden? That's what I'm here for really. The plants are very interesting. Some of them are still used in medicines; like this one, for example."

"Oh, I know that one," said Connie, knowledgeably. "That's borage."

William was impressed. "However did you know that?"

"You told me, silly."

"Don't be daft. I've never seen you before."

"No of course not, but I've seen you; on the telly. I told you."

The people began to trickle into the healing garden and William wandered over towards them in case they wanted to ask any questions. Connie draped herself over Edna's garden seat and sat watching William as he took people round. He knew about all his plants and the history of their past use when the monks were the only doctors people could go to for help, although the country folk themselves knew which plants to use for common complaints. William warmed to his subject once he got started and Connie found herself having to chat to her friends on her mobile to help pass the time until William got around to talking to her again.

"I can see this house is empty," said Connie. "The windows are all boarded up, so how are you going to look after your garden when the fence is put back?"

"That's the trouble; it's not my garden. The house is going to be sold, so my Dad says, and then I shall lose the garden I suppose but I hope they'll leave a small space round the side so I can get through. I shall have to ask Venus."

"You know Venus, then?"

"Of course I do. She's a part of the team who are making the programme. She was the one who asked me if I'd plant the garden and look after it. My Mum suggested it because Edna, who used to live here, was too old and muddled, and anyway I needed the money."

"Benji is my Dad's second cousin; that's why we came today; to meet the family."

"Oh, so you didn't come on your own."

"No, my family are all round talking to Venus and Benji. They'll be here soon and then I'll have to go but we're coming back to the barbecue in the evening after the awards have been given out. Benji's just asked us to come."

William hadn't intended to go to the celebration barbecue. He imagined they would all be old fogies there and as he didn't have a girlfriend to take he was going to disappear and go out on the town with his mates once the filming was finished. The situation looked a bit different now and he changed his mind. If Connie was going to be there then he would be there too.

Connie's family came into the garden, a noisy, happy crowd, and William showed them round, while Connie stuck firmly to his side.

"See you at the barbecue," shouted Connie, as they left.

"I'll be there," promised William.

It had been the most marvellous day. He seemed to have acquired a girlfriend out of the blue, and what a girlfriend! One who looked like a model and who had come just to see *him*! William found it hard to believe his luck.

CHAPTER 17

After the penultimate programme had been shown in its usual spot on Thursday the telephones became jammed with calls from voters until the lines were cut off. The response had been far more than Ed and his team had envisaged. Interest from the public was phenomenal. Ed's future as a director was assured and work on various projects would soon come pouring into the studio. Venus's idea had fired people's imaginations and Ed felt immensely grateful to her. There would always be a place for Venus on his team and he hoped she would stay now he had appointed her as his deputy director.

More people had watched the last programme than any other popular programme that evening and Ed felt justly proud of himself and all his team. The people who had visited the gardens and their friends and relations had all wanted to see if they could see themselves on the screen, and if anyone was caught on tape talking about the gardens that made it even better. As the programme began the opening shot taken from the helicopter had been changed to show the finished gardens and their owners waving skywards. The difference in the terrace was remarkable. Edna's tip had been turned into a recognisable garden, and everywhere there was a blaze of colour with the flowers and plants at their best.

The Hidden Gardens

The award ceremony took place on Saturday, at Number 6 Park Close where it had all begun, but this time the residents gathered in the garden. Ed stood on the decking of Benji's barbecue area to address the assembled company who were busy looking round to see if there was a famous face amongst them whom they could recognise.

"I have an apology to make," began Ed. "I'm sorry to say that the gardening expert we invited has been unable to come due to unforeseen circumstances, but someone else whom you all know very well has kindly agreed to take their place."

There was a groan of disappointment from everyone who had been discussing which famous gardening expert it was going to be. Most of them had expected Alan Titchmarsh to arrive although Malcolm was secretly hoping it would be that gorgeous woman whom he had watched on gardening programmes; the one with the big breasts. She could show him how to fix a water feature in his garden at any time, as long as she left her bra at home! Malcolm was her number one fan; not that she was to know that.

At this point Venus led an elderly lady onto the platform, dressed in a long skirt and a frilly white blouse, with her hair neatly secured under a wide band. At first nobody recognised her apart from Millie.

"It's Edna, isn't it?" she whispered to Mike. "She looks so different in those clothes; almost like the person who used to live in the end house when I was a child and yet I never recognised her."

"We asked Edna to come and present the awards," said Venus, "and she has kindly agreed to do so. None of us knew the garden at Number 12 belonged to her when we took over and turned it into a healing garden so we thought it would put the record straight if we asked her on this occasion, and I'm sure you all approve." Venus turned to face Edna, and took her hand. "It's really lovely to have you here with us today, Edna."

There was an element of surprise amongst the residents, as they looked at the neat and tidy elderly woman who bore no resemblance to the Edna they remembered, apart from the copious old straw bag from which she refused to be parted.

Benji helped Scrumpi onto the decking to give Edna a large bouquet of flowers, which Edna immediately pushed into her bag as if they might disappear at any moment. Everyone clapped politely, and Edna smiled with the sheer joy of seeing Scrumpi again, whom she obviously loved. Venus led her to a chair and sat beside her with Scrumpi on her lap. In case it all became too much for Edna, she was taking her back home after the winner had been presented with the cup.

"Why don't they get on with it," grumbled Malcolm, who was tired of waiting for the results to be announced.

"There were over a hundred thousand votes, you will be pleased to hear," said Ed. "Your efforts were watched by more people than you could imagine; far more than bothered to pick up a telephone and vote. The team would like to thank you all for your co-operation in helping to make the programme such a resounding success; and also to thank Beatrice Thorn who helped to create your gardens and to thank Julian Goodwood, who cannot be with us today, for the designs."

Malcolm's grumbling, urging Ed to finish with the preliminaries was becoming more audible and began to annoy the people around him, who tried to shut him up.

"I'm aware that some people can't wait for the result," said Ed, looking hard at Malcolm and raising a laugh at his expense, "but I want to mention one more thing which is the book about the series. Mr Wentworth is selling it in his Westminster bookshop as soon as it is published, and if you would like to order a copy he will be pleased to bring one home for you, at a reduced price."

"Huh!" snorted Malcolm, loud enough for Damian who was standing close by to hear. "You know we'll all buy one and you'll still make a good profit I'll bet!"

Damian felt uncomfortable and moved away, closely followed by Linda who glared angrily at her husband.

Ed chose to ignore him. "And now for the results," he continued, "there was a tie for fifth place between the rose garden at Number 2 and this garden at Number 6. Fourth place went to the healing garden at Number 12, which William made on his own with a little help from Beatrice, and third place goes to the

The Hidden Gardens

Persian garden at Number 8." Everyone clapped with enthusiasm as each result was announced. Malcolm held his breath, but Beatrice looked full of confidence. She was sure she had won.

"We needed a recount for the first and second place but by a very small margin the winner is Malcolm at Number 10, and the second prize goes to the Japanese garden at Number 4."

Beatrice looked angry; she should have won the first prize. She knew why this had happened; it was all the fault of that beastly Japanese man who had upset poor Ruth. A few days after the gardens had been opened she had seen a notice on a paper bill board in front of the paper shop in the parade. '*Disaster at local Japanese Garden,*' she read. As far as she knew her garden was the only Japanese garden in the area. Beatrice had gone in and bought a paper and was horrified to see a photograph of Ruth in a distressed state on the wooden bridge. Her hair was awry and her face looked like a clowns' with black streaks running down it while the samisen was lying broken in her hand. Someone who had been a late visitor to the garden must have taken the photograph unknown to Ruth and sold it to the newspaper; probably while she was off chasing that dreadful Japanese man. The photograph had been aptly named '*The Bridge of Sighs*' and there was a short report about the open gardens and another photograph of the Persian garden, but there was no explanation of Ruth's unhappiness. Beatrice had decided not to show it to her. There was no point in rubbing salt into the wound.

A few days later a huge and most expensive bouquet of Japanese irises, lilies and mimosa arrived at number 4, Park Close for the geisha girl, with a card from *The Pearl of the Orient Restaurant* and the one word—'*Apologies.*'

Ruth had wanted to throw them out immediately, knowing who had sent them but Beatrice had persuaded her to put them in water. They were too exquisite to throw away. However the damage had been done and Beatrice felt sure the newspaper article had put some people off voting for her garden. Nobody would have recognised Ruth but she had been portrayed as a figure of fun in the photograph and it had taken away from the whole conception of her project.

Jan Pollard

Ed handed Edna a silver tray to give to Beatrice, and Edna managed to say "Well done", when prompted by Venus, although it was obvious she wanted to stuff the tray into her old straw bag with the bouquet and not to pass it over which resulted in a few smiles from the onlookers.

Beatrice was gracious in defeat, but Malcolm behaved like a lunatic when he received the cup, dancing up and down and kissing it in front of the cameras, as if he was a member of a famous football team, and terrifying Edna as a result.

Everyone received a special framed certificate for taking part and there were congratulations all round. It was such a happy occasion that nobody felt as if they had lost out.

"We're inviting you all to a celebration barbecue this evening," said Venus. "It's a family party and for everyone who took part in the making of the programme, and that means *everyone*! Bring your families; the more the merrier. It's going to be a wonderful evening and Benji has prepared lots of food."

Ruth and Beatrice tendered their apologies. The school term was over and Ruth had received her leaving cheque from the staff and governors. They were due to be picked up by a taxi and taken to Heathrow to catch their evening flight to Tokyo after which they would take the bullet train to Kyoto where they would begin their holiday.

As they left the garden at Number 6 Ruth noticed Mike and Millie were holding hands.

"You see," she said to Beatrice. "I was right. He *was* having an affair with her all the time."

"What does it matter now, my dear. We have each other and the world is our oyster. He will be gone by the time we return. That part of your life is over; forget it and look to the future. In a few hours time we will be in Kyoto. Just imagine that!"

Damian had decided to opt out of the barbecue as well, and also proffered his apologies. It would be noisy and all of Benji and Venus's relations would be there, and there would be sure to be plenty of children if the ones who had visited his garden the other day was anything to go by. Somehow Damian thought it wouldn't be his scene. He would sit in his gazebo and play his

The Hidden Gardens

tape of bird song when it was all over and a bit quieter. In the meantime there was the television to look at where a good programme on civilisations was being shown, and he had a couple of new books to read. Linda had told him she was going out with a friend that evening. It was surprising how many friends she seemed to have; she was always going out in the evenings with one or the other of them, although they never seemed to come to the house for her. She dressed in very strange clothes for these occasions; black leather trousers, a leather jacket and a brightly patterned helmet. Damian presumed this friend owned a motorbike although he had never met him. She set off on foot so he supposed she met her friend at the end of Park Close where Malcolm would be unlikely to see her for which Damian felt thankful. The very idea of Malcolm landing up on his doorsteps in a rage gave him the shudders. Her private life was her own and as long as it never interfered with his he had no complaints. She was everything he could wish for in a housekeeper apart from a few minor details such as dusting, as she skirted round his ornaments, and her cooking, which was a bit hit and miss, but she was a kind, generous person and a loyal servant. It was all he wanted from a companion and he considered himself a happy man. One couldn't have everything in this life, as he had found with Guy.

Malcolm made tracks for the pub as soon as he had received his award. His mates would all be gathered there to see if he had won, as the final programme wouldn't be shown until the next Thursday. He took the silver cup and placed it in pride of place on the bar for all to see so he could drink the beers they bought him out of his trophy. Malcolm was in his element. The fact that some of them had telephoned in their votes twenty or thirty times so he would win made no difference to Malcolm. If they expected him to buy them drinks they were mistaken. This was his night and he expected to be fêted by everyone who came into the pub that evening and to get roaring drunk before he was turned out.

There was only one member of the maintenance gang who was not coming that evening and he had been the last one to join. Malcolm was told that he had a hot date and would not be there. Malcolm felt no bad feelings towards him for not coming, although things might have been different had he known that the hot date was his wife Linda, and Malcolm raised his silver cup and gave a toast to absent friends, wherever they might be. William put on a clean pair of denims, which he had difficulty in finding, and a purple silk blouse, which his mother had left behind. He liked the effect. The blouse was too big and came out over the top of his jeans making him look trendy, a bit like a pop star in his opinion. There was a short gold chain with a medallion in her dressing table drawer and he tried that on too and considered it looked quite fetching. The fact that it was a Saint Christopher medal was of little consequence. Connie would never see what was on it; she would be too busy getting to know him better, or so he hoped. He sat and watched a programme on the television for something to do until it was time to go round to Number 6. He was so churned up inside about seeing Connie again that he had to keep going to the lavatory, and the T.V. programme could have been about Tibetan monks for all the notice that he took of it. In fact it was a travel programme called *'Wish you were here'* which meant nothing to William who wanted to be somewhere else but it helped to pass the time.

At six o'clock on the dot he presented himself on the front doorstep of Number 6 only to discover that he was the first one to arrive.

Venus, who hardly recognised him, was surprised to see him so early.

"Hallo William; there's nobody here yet. How about giving Benji a helping hand? He's just got the barbecue going and he could do with a second chef."

She smiled broadly as she ushered the unenthusiastic William into the garden.

"Hi there, William, you're just the man I need. Will you skewer those prawns onto the kebabs and dip them into the marinade ready for cooking? That's great!"

William could see nothing for it and got on with the job hoping that Connie would soon make an appearance as the prawns kept slipping off the skewers much to his annoyance. He began to wonder why Benji had become a chef, especially as after all this fiddling about everything was eaten in a few minutes. He intended to get a job as a gardener or work in a garden centre when he had left the comprehensive next year, and hoped that his part in the programme would be a recommendation for such work. He mentioned it to Benji, as they busied themselves with the preparations.

"Hey, man! Watch them prawns! They're trying to get back into the sea!"

William had laughed and had tried to be more careful. Benji was a right funny bloke.

"Well, I'm sure Venus would give you a good reference, and so would Ed; don't you forget to ask when the time comes; but I'm not giving you a reference for a chef's job: no way, man!"

He gave William a hearty slap on the back and a few more prawns bit the dust. William picked them up and skewered them on while Benji was otherwise occupied.

At long last people began to arrive and much to his relief, William was released from his culinary duties.

Mike and Millie arrived with Lucy, who was worried that none of her friends would be there, but as soon as the reggae music started and the other West Indian families arrived with their children, Lucy was swept away by the others and danced along to the rhythm with everyone else. Mike and Millie wandered amongst the flower borders, drinking Benji's special ginger-rum punch. Benji had placed lights amongst the flowers to reflect their bright colours and give the garden a magical glow under the night sky. For Millie this was just the beginning of a night when all her dreams were to come true, and she hoped they could soon slip away and leave Lucy there for a while.

Connie arrived in a sparkling gold two piece which left her mid riff bare and one leg uncovered and danced her way across to William, encouraging him to join her as she moved to the rhythm. When it grew darker the lights amongst the flowers formed pools of moving colours as the shadows of the dancers passed across them. After a few hours the film crew melted away. Ed stayed a little longer to chat to the staff from the studios and their families who had been invited and then he left too. It was only a small garden and everyone wanted a share in the fun. Benji danced on his rostrum, waving his spatula as he turned the food on the barbecue. In his white apron and his cook's hat he looked as if he was conducting an orchestra as the dancers whirled round him, intoxicated by the beauty of the garden and the copious glasses of his rum punch.

Venus found Mike and Millie at the end of the garden behind the trees, their arms around each other, kissing passionately. She had come to replenish their glasses but had decided not to disturb them when Millie caught sight of her.

"It's a magical evening, Venus. Thank you so much for making it possible. It was the best idea you've ever had, believe me."

"More punch?" asked Venus, with a broad smile.

"I think we've had enough, thanks," said Mike, "almost too much."

Millie giggled. "We're going home now Venus, but we'll leave Lucy for a while longer as she's having such a good time, if you don't mind."

Venus gave them a knowing look. She could see how it was; they needed to be on their own together, to make love. Well, good luck to them both. His hard faced wife had left for a holiday with Beatrice and these two obviously had something going between them.

"She can stay the night if you like. Some of the other kids are having what they call a sleepover and have brought their sleeping bags. I can find her a couple of blankets. I'll tell Lucy, if you like, and I'll keep an eye on her. She'll be fine here although I doubt the kids will get much sleep to-night."

"Bless you, Venus; you're a good friend," said Millie, as they made their way out of the garden. She could see Venus speaking to Lucy as they left, and gave her a wave. Lucy waved back briefly and continued to have fun with her new friends. The night belonged to them, a night made for love.

The Hidden Gardens

"Isn't there a place where we can be alone?" asked Connie, who wanted William to herself. "What about your garden? I've got something to tell you."

"You'll have to squeeze through the fence."

"I can squeeze through anything, with a bit of help from you."

William and Connie walked round to the front of Edna's house, and along the side passage and found the slit in the fence which had been left for William so he could continue to water the plants until the house was sold.

"I'll tear my skirt getting through that. I'll have to take it off. You don't mind do you?"

William raised no objections. In fact he welcomed seeing a bit more of Connie's legs.

Once inside they sat on Edna's seat and Connie wrapped herself around him and kissed him for a long time. William was only too happy to do the same to her for as long as she felt like it.

"Have you had a lot of girlfriends, William?" asked Connie, coming up for breath.

"Hundreds," lied, William. "They queue up for me; night after night."

"I'm not surprised. You're very good at snogging."

"Mind you, I'll put them off now I've found you. You're the best of the lot."

Connie sighed, contently.

"My Dad hopes to buy this house; that's what I wanted to tell you. He buys up old property and does it up with my uncles. Then they sell at a large profit. So you can keep the garden, William, until it gets sold again. Of course it might not get sold for ages and then you can keep on looking after the garden. I'll come and help you with it if you like. I'm going to live with Venus and Benji soon and look after their little girl so we shall see a lot of each other. Venus is having another baby so she'll need a lot of help."

"Wicked!" said William amazed at this revelation.

Jan Pollard

He didn't think much gardening would be done while Connie was around. She was too much of a distraction.

"I don't leave the comprehensive 'til next year; how about you?"

"I've left already. I'm moving in next week."

William gave a low whistle. She was some girl.

"Benji thinks I can get such good references that I should be able to get a job at a garden centre. I'll see what I can do this summer; get a holiday job in a place like that and then get taken on next spring, if I'm lucky!"

"There you are then; we'll be living almost next door to each other."

This time it was William who wrapped himself around her and began to make love to her, which was more successful than he could ever have imagined. There had to be a first time for everything and Connie had shown him how easy it could be. William thought she was wonderful until a sudden thought struck him.

"You on the pill, Con?" At sixteen the idea of fatherhood, and all that involved alarmed him. Look what had happened to his sister and the rows at home when his parents had found out.

"Course I am; I'm always prepared for anything."

William could believe that, and sighed with relief.

CHAPTER 18

The children had fallen asleep at last. Venus had begun to think they would never stop whispering and giggling. They were all too excited to sleep, that was the trouble.

She rolled over and told Benji to close his mouth in a stage whisper. He was snoring like a pig and she would never get any sleep if that continued. Benji gave a snort and closed his mouth and peace reigned at last.

Venus looked up at the ceiling. It had been the best idea she had ever had. It had made a lot of money for the television company and Ed was well pleased. They would put off leaving for a year or two now she was having another baby. Connie was coming to look after Scrumpi so she could go on working for a while longer, and anyway the terrace had become a much friendlier place since the makeover, and they had a wonderful garden into the bargain. Her eyes began to close and Venus drifted off to sleep at last with a huge smile of contentment on her face.

The lovers at Number 2 were lying in each other's arms in a passionate embrace. Sleep was still a long way off.

Millie had arranged a bed of rugs and cushions in Lucy's secret garden, where the scent of the roses would surround them as they made love. A bottle of champagne was keeping cool in the little water feature, surrounded by ice. Mike had laughed when he had first seen it; nobody but Millie could have thought of such a thing.

He had waited patiently for her while she went to change into a black lace negligee. She had stood for a moment bathed in the moonlight and the negligee had fallen to the ground as he had taken her into his arms. She was even more beautiful in her nakedness and Mike kissed every part of her until passion overtook them both and they lay together under the stars in an ecstasy of love.

Somewhere there was a nightingale singing but they were far too preoccupied to wonder where the sound was coming from, or even to notice when the singing came to an abrupt end, as Damian turned off his tape.

ACKNOWLEDGEMENTS

My thanks to the members of the Romantic Novelists' Association, for all their fellowship, encouragement and helpful critiques of my writing, and especially to the author, the late Joan Hessayon, for her introduction to the Association. Also to Dr. Dave Hessayon for making us feel so welcome on the occasions of our visits to his beautiful garden at Sloe House.

My many thanks to my family for their patience and assistance and to my editor Mike Pomerantz for bringing my writing to a successful conclusion.